DREAMWORKS

the **BAD GUYS**

Movie Novelization

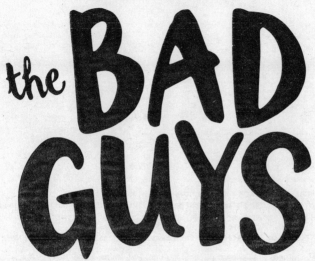

DreamWorks

the **BAD GUYS**

Movie Novelization

By Kate Howard

Scholastic Inc.

ISBN 978-1-338-74569-6

10 9 8 7 6 5 4 3 2 1   22 23 24 25 26

Printed in the U.S.A.   40

First printing 2022

Book design by Jess Meltzer

Stock photos © Shutterstock.com

PROLOGUE

Hey, you. Yeah, you. Get over here.

Now come a little closer. Are you afraid? Because I'm the, uh . . . BIG BAD WOLF? You think I'm a monster? Not surprised. I *am* the villain in every story. But I'm here to tell you that names—and reputation and looks (yeah, even sometimes good looks, like mine)—can be deceiving.

Got your attention now, don't I?

Curious to know what I'm talking about? Well, I'm here to tell you about the greatest adventure of all time. If you haven't already figured it out from the name on the cover, they call me and my friends the Bad Guys, and we're the stars of this adventure. The story I'm about to tell you started almost exactly a year ago, on my pal Snake's birthday. It all began the way every good story should begin . . . with a tasty meal and great friends.

Read on, and I'll see you on the flip side.

CHAPTER ONE

The diner was quieter than usual, considering there should have been the afternoon rush. As always, Wolf and his buddy, Snake, had gotten their favorite table—the very best window booth—and the service was quick. Maybe even quicker than usual. They were just finishing up their meal, noisily chomping and slurping the very last dregs of their food and coffee, while debating an ever-important topic of conversation that came around exactly once each year: Snake's birthday.

"Forget about it," Snake told Wolf.

"Yeah," Wolf said, nodding slowly. "But it's weird!"

"Stop," Snake insisted.

"Fine," Wolf said, wiping his mouth with one hairy paw. "I'll stop asking about it if you just explain it to me."

Snake glared at his friend across the table. *This conversation is getting old*, he thought. "There's nothing to explain," he muttered. He was tired of talking about his birthday. What he really wanted was to grab a nice, wiggly, rodent dessert and get back to his favorite subject: their next Bad Guy heist. There was nothing he loved as much as stealing stuff. "Would you please drop it?"

"Consider it dropped," Wolf said, holding up his hands in surrender. "I promise. It's dropped." He gestured to the floor and said, "It's on the ground." He looked at his plate, trying hard to let it go. But he just couldn't understand Snake's reluctance to talk about *his big day*. Birthdays meant attention, and presents, and friends, and all kinds of other fun stuff. He snuck a peek at his pal and cried out, "But come on! Everybody loves birthdays. You've got decorations, balloons, parties . . . and CAKE." He smiled his most charming smile, but it wasn't enough to crack through his grouchy pal's sour expression.

Snake hissed. "I don't *need* presents, I don't *want* decorations, and I'm *not* a cake guy." He gazed out the window, watching as people hustled to work and out for coffee meetings. Across the street was Snake's favorite view: the "Big Bank," which was also known as "The Bad Guys' Next Target." If there was one thing that could cheer him up, it was the prospect of stealing stuff.

But Wolf didn't want to talk about that—his mind was stuck on one thing, and one thing only. Heists were everyday affairs; birthdays only came around once a year. "Seriously, though," he persisted. "You don't like cake? Name one food better than cake."

"Guinea pig," Snake replied, without even having to think about it. There was just something about swallowing down his favorite rodent treat that made him feel so, so good.

Wolf collapsed back against the booth. "Again with the guinea pigs! C'mon! I bet if I blindfolded you, you wouldn't be able to tell the difference between a skunk and a guinea pig."

"Wrong," Snake snapped back. "Snakes have impeccable taste buds. I can taste air." He stuck his tongue out, letting his forked, air-tasting tongue do its job. He could taste the syrup stuck to the booth a few tables over and could make out the slightest hint of a mushroom and bacon sandwich.

"Air?" Wolf asked, laughing.

"Yes, air," Snake said haughtily. He stuck his tongue out again. "Mmm, nice!" But with another flick of his tongue, Snake suddenly tasted that the diner's soup of the day was obviously split pea. He pulled his tongue back in before he could get a bigger taste of *that*. Guinea pig stew he could handle, but the smell of split pea was enough to ruin his appetite.

"I don't know," Wolf said, draping one furry arm up and over the back of the booth. "Guinea pigs are just a little, uh, *cute* for my taste."

"That's what makes them so delicious!" Snake said. "You're not just eating food, you're eating pure *goodness*. It's not about the pig, it's about what it symbolizes on a deeper level!"

Wolf nodded slowly, clearly considering this argument. "So . . . you can actually *taste* air? What else you got?"

Snake rolled his eyes. "Ugh, forget about it."

Wolf looked excited about this new information. *It is always nice*, he thought, *to get to know my buddy on a deeper level.* That's what friendship was all about. "Can you also hear color? Can you see sound?" He leaned forward, his paws on the table. "'Cause we should really be capitalizing on these skills."

Snake drooped in the booth, waiting for his friend's enthusiasm to run its course. "Fine," he said dryly. "Get it all out—get it all out now." Just then, a muffled beeping sound came from somewhere nearby.

Beep.

Beep.

Beep beep.

Snake coughed, and an alarm clock came tumbling out of his mouth. He hit a button, silencing the beeping, and glanced at the clock face. "It's four o'clock. Now I know the exact moment our friendship died." He swallowed the alarm clock back down again.

Wolf laughed. Snake could *pretend* to be a grouch, but Wolf knew there was a soft underbelly on him somewhere. Wolf patted the table. "Let's bounce." As they pushed their plates and coffee cups away, Wolf let his own long tongue hang out the side of his mouth. He lifted his eyes to the ceiling and held up one finger. "It tastes like . . . like you're going to stick me with the bill. Again."

Snake smirked. "Well, it *is* my birthday."

"So *now* you play the birthday card," Wolf said, chuckling. "That's interesting."

While they waited for the waitress to swing past, Wolf flashed a charismatic smile out into the restaurant—but then realized there was no one smiling back. In fact, there was no one sitting at *any* of the other tables, and none of the waitstaff were milling about the restaurant. It was like a ghost town. Wolf used his extra keen sight to take a closer look and noticed a group of women huddled behind the counter, trying to hide. There were a few people tucked into a corner, very obviously hoping to not make eye contact with him. On closer inspection, he realized there were people hidden *everywhere* around the diner. It was always like this—people spotted him and his friends, and they hid like nervous prairie dogs.

Wolf held up a finger, signaling for the check. "Check, please? Hello?" He whistled and flashed another wolfish grin. "The . . . checkity-check?" No one moved a muscle. He could feel the fear in the air, and he guessed his friend Snake could probably *taste* it. "You know what?" Wolf called out to whoever was listening. "We're just gonna leave the money here." He counted out a few bills and slipped them onto the table, but no one yelled out "Thanks," or "Sounds good," or acknowledged him in any way.

Man, he thought, *service is really going down the toilet in this place*.

"You know the one good thing about this place?" Snake asked as they stood up and started to head for the door.

"What?"

Snake shrugged as though it were obvious. It kind of *was* obvious. "We never have to wait for a table."

"Isn't that *every* place?" Wolf reminded him.

Snake turned to a group of customers who were cowering in a corner, hoping not to be noticed. He tipped his chin and said, "Hey, man, how have you been? I haven't seen you in forever." Then, for good measure, he hissed, *"Snake attack!"* Doing that always gave him a laugh. Before they got to the door, Snake hissed at all the other losers huddled into corners and under tables. Everyone scrambled to hide deeper in the shadows, shaking with fear.

"Ooh!" Snake whooped as they passed the front register. "Mints!" He swallowed the whole thing down, including the bowl.

"Sorry, folks," Wolf called out to the other restaurant patrons, trying to make nice. They were criminals, the Bad

Guys, but that didn't mean they had to be bad *guys*. "I'm switching him to decaf."

Snake slithered to the door and pushed it open, exiting into the busy afternoon. "Okay," he called over his shoulder. "Let's do this."

CHAPTER TWO

Outside, the two legendary criminals strolled down the sidewalk side by side. All around them, people veered away and skittered to hide their faces—the Bad Guys were well-known, and highly feared. Cars and trucks screeched to a halt, making it easy for the two to cross the street to the front doors of the Big Bank.

"Guinea pigs, huh?" Wolf asked again. Seemed like an odd choice for a favorite snack. Who would pick a tiny little rodent over a nice, sweet piece of birthday cake?

"They're the Rolls-Royce of rodents," Snake said, flicking his tongue. All this talk of rodents was making him hungry—even though they'd just finished lunch. But then again, Snake was *always* up for a snack.

"Yeah," Wolf said, shaking his head. "But still a *rodent*. You know what I mean?"

Outside the Big Bank, the two friends admired the posters hanging on the building's windows. There were dozens of **WANTED** posters, all featuring Mr. Wolf and Mr. Snake's mug shots. Wolf nodded appreciatively—it felt so good to be known.

"Don't mind us," Wolf said, flashing a charming smile at one of the people they passed as they strolled through the bank's massive front doors. "Just robbin' this place."

As soon as they were inside, tucked safely into the air-conditioned building full of money, Wolf and Snake switched into autopilot. They'd pulled off so many of these heists over the years, it was almost *too* easy to do a job like this. Now, as they strolled up to the teller, the two Bad Guys each bared their razor-sharp fangs and Wolf flashed his knifelike claws. The bank teller froze for a second, then screamed— loud and long—as soon as he realized what was happening. It was any bank employee's worst nightmare.

"**Aaaaaahhhhhwoooooolfffff!**" the teller shrieked, backing away from the thieves. Snake could tell that the employee's whole body was shaking. After so many heists, watching people's fear come alive was one of the best parts of the job. It was always a version of the same situation. They came in, the person being robbed screamed or went pale or ran, and the Bad Guys took the cash. Easy peasy.

Today, Wolf and Snake shared an amused look, then grabbed the bank's giant safe from behind the counter. In the next second, they fled. Everything was going exactly according to plan. The two friends exploded out the side windows of the bank and tossed the giant safe into the back of their Bad Guys' car.

The car was Wolf's pride and joy, a gorgeous sports car fit for celebrities—celebrities like the Bad Guys! "Woo!" Wolf whooped, sliding into the driver's seat. Snake slid into the passenger's seat beside him, the safe snuggled in right on Snake's lap. "Yeah!"

"Hahaha!" Snake cheered. They'd outsmarted the good guys, once again.

"Go bad . . ." Wolf started, his smile spreading across his face.

"Or go home," Snake finished.

Wolf pressed the gas pedal and floored it. Zipping through the streets of Los Angeles, Wolf felt lighter than air. They had cash for days, his best friend was at his side trying to crack a new safe they'd just stolen, and the cops were hot on their tail. There was no better—or more satisfying—way to spend an afternoon.

While Snake worked on cracking the safe open, Wolf expertly guided the Bad Guy mobile through the streets. "Serpentine safe-cracking machine," Wolf mused, glancing over to watch his friend work. "I like to imagine Houdini—but with no arms. The kinda guy who'll tell you the glass is half empty—then steal it from you." He grinned at Snake, then veered around another crop of slowed and stopped cars. Wolf continued to narrate their drive, as he zigged and zagged around traffic. "He's also my best bud. And today is . . . his birthday!"

Snake glanced up from the safe. "Not relevant. In this moment, or ever."

"He's a sweetheart," Wolf called out to someone in a passing car. Then he smirked at his friend and said it directly to him, "You're a sweetheart, you know that?"

Behind them, a parade of police cars filed into position, swerving and dodging pedestrians in their quest to *finally* catch this pair of legendary criminals in the act.

"Well, look who's here," Snake mused, glancing back at the cops giving chase. It was always just a matter of time until police were on their tail . . . and then just a matter of a little *more* time before the Bad Guys got away.

"Took 'em long enough." Wolf laughed. He scanned the road ahead, noticing a long string of red lights, with tons of traffic in every direction. There was no way they would get through that mess—without some help. Luckily, they had help. "Watch this: Three . . . two . . . one!"

Suddenly, the lights switched from red to green, ushering

the Bad Guys through the jammed streets with ease. Wolf gave a little salute to their hacker pal—Tarantula—who was perched on a streetlight overhead. "Our in-house hacker," Wolf cheered. "Our pocket search engine, our traveling tech wizard." He pumped a fist, then in an announcer's voice, added, "We call her . . . WEBS."

While the guys had done *their* thing and stolen the goods, Tarantula had been busy doing her thing: working on hacking the city's streetlight system to grant them easy passage during their getaway. Now, as the Bad Guys drove under her perch on the streetlight, Webs jumped down and dropped into the Bad Guy mobile.

For Webs, this had been a simple job. A basic hack. Nothing complicated. She was a total perfectionist and also preferred to juggle many tasks at once. And having eight legs made tackling multiple jobs at any given time a little easier. The best part of *this* particular hack? As soon as the Bad Guys drove through the green lights, the stoplights immediately switched back to *red*, stopping all the cars behind them and letting the cars going the *other* direction go. This clogged up all the intersections and kept the cop cars who'd been chasing them from getting through!

"Very slick, Webs," Wolf said admiringly.

"I also took over the police dispatch," Webs bragged. "Blurred their satellite imaging system, grounded their chopper, and . . ." She paused, glancing back over her shoulder. "One more thing."

Just then, a delivery driver on a scooter pulled up alongside their getaway car.

Snake glanced over, groaning as he realized what his friend had done. "You didn't."

Webs snickered.

The delivery driver hollered out, "Special delivery for . . ." He glanced up, suddenly realizing who his clients were. **"Ahhhh!** Don't eat me!!" He flung the package toward the car, his scooter swerving as he freaked out about how close he'd been to the legendary Bad Guys.

Webs calmly reached up and caught the package with a free leg. Beside her, Snake grimaced at the sight of the giant birthday cake his friend had delivered to their getaway car. "Happy birthday, Mr. Grumpypants," Tarantula cooed.

Snake looked from the cake to Wolf and back to Webs in frustration. "I think I hate you," he told Webs.

Wolf was feeling better than ever as he turned left to lead the few remaining cops toward a construction zone. Their plan was still going exactly according to . . . well, according to plan. As they drove through the construction site, as soon as they'd passed, one of the workers gestured for a crane to lower a port-a-potty into the middle of the street. This blocked all but a small handful of the remaining cop cars.

Only a few left to ditch, and they'd be home free.

As the Bad Guys' car zipped past the construction worker, another one of the Bad Guys—Mr. Shark—hopped into the car beside his teammates. "Guys! It's me!" Shark said joyfully as he shed his uniform disguise. "I was the construction worker!"

"Mr. Shark," Wolf said, offering his pal a huge smile and cheering. "Master of Disguise! Our apex predator of a thousand faces."

Shark grinned, soaking up the praise and attention. He loved being part of the Bad Guys, and he really *was* a master of disguise. His greatest trick of all? Stealing the *Mona Lisa* disguised *as* the Mona Lisa. It was a true highlight in his heisting career.

With Shark now squeezed into the backseat, things had gotten a bit squishy in the car. Shark was significantly bigger than the other Bad Guys and took up far more than his fair share of space.

"Watch it, Big Tuna," Snake hissed as Shark wiggled into his spot—which shoved Snake's seat forward and pressed him against the safe he was still working to crack. "I'm trying to work here!"

Shark relaxed into his seat. "Keep it cool, baby. Birthdays should be chill." He pulled out a birthday hat and candles, doing his own part to keep Snake's birthday celebration going full swing. Birthdays only came around once a year, so Shark, like Wolf and Webs, felt like they deserved a major celebration. He shoved the candles into the cake and tied the party hat around Snake's slim head.

Snake's head drooped under the weight of the hat, and his mood drooped with it. "You do realize we're in the middle of a chase, right?"

Shark glanced back, noticing with only the slightest concern that the cops on their tail had drawn dangerously close to their getaway car. It was time to put the pedal to the metal, or they'd be caught!

But based on Wolf's wolfish grin, there was one last trick up his sleeve. "And rounding out the crew . . ." he said as he swerved the wheel to throw one of the cop cars offtrack. He glanced in the rearview mirror just in time to see the glove box of one of the police cars *pop* open, revealing the final member of their team.

"Surprise!" Mr. Piranha shouted, leaping into the face of the nearest cop. He flipped and flopped around the inside of the police car like a Tasmanian devil, causing the car to swerve off course. At the precise moment, Piranha jumped out the window into another cop car. He jumped from cop car to cop car—causing mass chaos.

"He's a loose cannon with a short fuse," Wolf cried out, watching his pal do his best work. "Willing to scrap with anyone or anything." Behind them, Piranha continued to leap and jump in the air, now landing on the roofs of each of the cars pursuing the Bad Guys. "He's brave . . ." Wolf continued announcing. "He's

fearless . . ." Eventually, Piranha bounced onto the windshield of the lead cop car, freaking out the driver, who slammed on his brakes and caused a massive pileup. "Who am I kidding? He's crazy!"

Moments later, Piranha pinballed up and through the air, landing in the Bad Guy mobile.

"*Santo cielo*," Piranha whooped. "That's a lot of *popo*!"

"Piranha," Tarantula said slowly, "did you forget something?"

"Uhhh . . ." Piranha said, looking around nervously. He'd been pretty sure he'd taken care of all the cops in hot pursuit, but maybe he'd missed one? *Nah.*

"The present . . ." Shark prompted. He gestured toward Snake, still hard at work on the safe in the front seat.

"Oh! Um, of course I didn't forget . . ." Piranha said hastily, covering for himself. He'd totally forgotten the present. As his friends shot daggers at him with their eyes, Piranha ripped a tiny fart.

Webs shook her head. "You know, you fart when you lie."

Piranha cowered under her stare. "I fart when I'm nervous."

"Yeah," Webs countered. "Nervous about lying!"

Unable to stop it from happening, Piranha launched another fart—but this time it was a giant, silent-but-deadly one. Within seconds, the entire car filled with noxious green gas.

"PIRANHA!" The rest of the Bad Guys screamed.

"Sorry . . ." Piranha squeaked.

"Don't breathe it in," Wolf reminded the others.

Shark started freaking out and flopped around in the backseat of the car. "I breathed it in!"

The rest of the Bad Guys coughed and stuck their heads out the windows, gasping for fresh air.

As soon as the gas dissipated inside the car, Wolf looked around at his crazy collection of friends and thought—once again—about how lucky he was. "Yeah, they're a bit eccentric," he muttered, continuing his little narration as the other Bad Guys continued to shriek and wail about the fart. "But," he said, chuckling, "when you're born *us*, friends don't exactly grow on trees. Do I wish people didn't see us as monsters?" he wondered aloud. "Sure . . . but these are the cards we've been dealt, so we might as well play 'em."

Just then, Snake successfully cracked the safe. It clicked open and Snake whooped with delight. "Jackpot!"

Wolf beamed at him. "Nice work, birthday boy."

Snake hissed back.

Laughing, Wolf spun the car and drifted into position right in front of the police station. The safe popped out in front of a gaggle of cops, who were all standing in front of the building. Every single pair of eyes turned to stare.

"What the thorax?!" Tarantula gasped.

"Are you crazy?" Piranha gurgled.

"What?" Wolf said, winking. "I just wanted a longer car chase. It's the best part."

The chief of police glared out the window. Beside her, one of the other cops said, "Chief . . . it's . . . it's . . ."

"THEM!" The chief screamed, her eyes widening to the size of dinner plates. She burst out the front doors of the station. She was going to get her mitts on those horrible criminals one of these days! It was her life's greatest ambition.

"Webs," Wolf said. "Hit it."

Tarantula pressed play on the stereo, and music blared out of the Bad Guy mobile.

"Get them!" the police chief screamed.

CHAPTER THREE

Dancing and singing along to the music, Wolf and his friends sped through the streets of Los Angeles. Behind them, a whole new fleet of cop cars had now joined the chase. The chief's car pulled up beside them, and she climbed out the window—she would do whatever it took to catch the Bad Guys! The chief grabbed the door of Wolf's car and pulled it toward her with tremendous strength.

Wolf's face broke into an even wider smile. There was nothing quite as satisfying as seeing frustration written all over his favorite police chief's face. And he had a *great* view of her face, seeing as she was hanging—suspended—between her own car and his, like a bridge.

"I'm going to put you guys away for so long, your fleas will have fleas!" She growled.

Shark leaned out the window. "Chief . . . you want some cake?" he offered. "You seem a little hangry."

The chief shouted back, "Get that thing out of my face before I—"

"Excuse me," Wolf cut her off. "Excuse me, Chief!"

"What?" The police chief sputtered.

Wolf gestured with his chin for the chief to take a look at the road ahead. While she'd been focusing on stopping the Bad Guy mobile, her own car had nearly sideswiped a bus! "Ahhhhhhhh!" she screamed, climbing back into her car and clutching the wheel just in time to prevent a collision.

"Uh," Piranha said, glancing nervously out the car's front window. "*Hermano* . . ." Wolf was driving straight toward a blockade of police cars. They were totally boxed in! But Wolf just kept accelerating as if he didn't see that there was nowhere for them to go but straight into the blockade.

"WOLLLFFF!" his pals screamed.

At the very last second, Wolf threw the steering wheel to the left and drove down a huge staircase. As they bumped down the stairs, all the Bad Guys flew out the sunroof, flipping and flopping in midair, before landing back in the car with a thud. And Snake's birthday cake had come out of the whole ordeal no worse for the wear . . .

"Yeah," Wolf muttered, pleased as punch about yet another perfectly executed heist. "We may be bad guys . . . but we're so *good* at it."

As the police cars crashed to a halt behind them, the chief climbed out of her car and growled when the Bad Guys disappeared into the sunset. "Not *again*," she fumed. "No! No!

No! No! No! Keep running, Wolf. One of these days, your luck is gonna run out."

Wolf had heard that line plenty of times before. Much as the chief liked to think she had the Bad Guys in her crosshairs, she just couldn't seem to catch them. And with Wolf's secret lair, they had a nice, comfy place to hide out until it was time for their next heist.

Now that they'd successfully dodged their way through a second cop chase, they headed for the lair. They zoomed into a river aqueduct, crossed through an abandoned tunnel, then finally arrived at an unmarked set of doors that opened automatically for them. Wolf steered the car into the parking lift, and the doors to the lair's entrance sealed up behind them.

Safe and sound at home, hidden among the streets of Los Angeles.

Inside Wolf's lair, all their prized, stolen possessions were on full display. The roomy loft had plenty of space to display jewels, cash, priceless works of art, and all the other treasures they'd acquired over the years. But today, the centerpiece of the whole place was the birthday spread set up in the kitchen. Balloons hung from the ceiling, signs calling out HAPPY BIRTHDAY, and a spot in the center of the table for Snake's tasty birthday cake.

Wolf bounced across the room to deliver the cake to its rightful spot. Everyone else gathered around, preparing to sing to their grumpy pal. "Alright, Piranha, you're up," Wolf said. He knew Snake wasn't *expecting* this, but who wouldn't *love* the chance to have everyone celebrate you?

In a surprisingly clear and lovely voice, Piranha began to sing. "Happy birthd—"

Piranha's voice sounded like an angel singing, but before he could even get through the first line of the classic birthday song, Snake blew out the candles on the cake and glared at his friends, immediately killing the mood and his pal's song.

"Seriously?" Tarantula groaned.

"C'mon, Snake," Wolf said, nudging the birthday guy. "At least make a toast!"

Snake sighed. "Okay, alright, listen. I've made a lot of enemies in my time. A *lot*. But out of all the people in the world, I hate you guys the least."

The other four were caught off-guard by this extreme compliment. Coming from Snake, that kind of sentiment meant a whole lot. "Awwww," Tarantula cooed.

Piranha began to tear up, overcome by his friend's emotional words. "That was actually kind of beautiful . . ."

Shark nodded. "You're a poet, man."

Wolf lifted his glass into the air while Snake crossed his nubby snake arms in defiance. "To Mr. Snake," Wolf cheered. "And his strange dislike of birthdays."

Wolf, Webs, Shark, and Piranha all cheered loudly while

Snake waved them off—he was totally overcome with embarrassment. Snake always hated this kind of attention.

As Wolf lifted his arms in front of them all, preparing to take a selfie to capture the big moment, he cried out, "Everyone say 'Robbery!'" He inspected the picture, grinning at the result. "Look at those dimples . . . happy birthday, buddy."

Snake gestured to the cake, perched like a prize in the center of the table. "Okay, now dig in, fellas." His four friends had all been staring hungrily at the cake for far too long, and he knew they couldn't wait to take a slice.

But before any of the others could react, Piranha buzzed through the cake, leaving only a sad-looking cake skeleton that collapsed before he had even wiped the leftover frosting off his fishy lips.

"Come on!" Wolf howled.

"Hey!" Shark moaned.

Tarantula stared at the empty cake plate in horror.

"You snooze, you lose." Piranha shrugged, smacking his mouth.

Across the room, Snake hardly even noticed the cake argument happening at the table. He was too busy sticking the newest group selfie on the fridge, admiring this one lined up next to all their other Bad Guy "family" photos. They'd really had some good times over the years, he and the guys. He reached into the freezer to grab his own favorite treat—a frozen push pop.

But before he could even open the thing, Shark popped up behind him and started moaning and drooling with hunger. "Ooh . . ." Shark moaned. "Push pops! Man, my tummy is rumbling like a kraken right now."

"Yeah," Snake knew the push pop was the last one in the box. And his friend wanted it . . . "Want one?"

Tarantula called out, "You know he's not going to give it to you, Shark."

Shark shook his head. "No, I believe that deep down, Snake is a kind and generous soul."

After a pause, Tarantula asked, "Why?"

Snake held out the pop, waving the icy treat in front of his friend's nose. "Here. Take it."

Shark grinned and opened his mouth wide. "Oh, yeah! Pop me, please!"

But before Shark could get even his first row of teeth on the push pop, Snake tossed it into his own gaping mouth and swallowed it whole. Laughing, he teased, "Sucker!"

"Come on, man," Shark whined. "Now you're gonna make me get all aggressive." He growled and pounced on his friend. The two Bad Guys began to brawl, fighting over a push pop that was now long gone.

Gazing fondly at his two best friends, fighting over an icy

treat like a couple of brothers, Wolf mused, "Aw, you guys are a bunch of animals." Wolf loved his gang of friends, and that love grew a little more every day. He knew he was lucky to have such incredible pals. He snapped on the TV, settling into the couch as he said, "Let's see what they're saying about us today."

On the TV, there was a banner that read: BREAKING NEWS! A young, ambitious news reporter named Tiffany Fluffit was standing in front of the massive police car pileup the Bad Guys had left in their wake not half an hour before. Tiffany had been eagerly waiting for her big break as a reporter, and it looked very much like she'd finally found it! "Tiffany Fluffit," she chirped into a microphone, "Channel Six Action News. The Bad Guys have struck again, with their most brazen heist yet! Proving once again that they are the most diabolical criminals of our time—"

"Guys," Wolf called out, trying to cut through the sounds of the push pop battle happening behind him. "Stop it! We're on TV." Everyone stopped fighting and crowded in around the couch to see what the news was reporting about them after today's bank robbery.

"Ooh, *diabolical*," Tarantula said, rubbing her eight legs together. "That's new."

"Sounds like a cologne." Shark giggled. He switched to a suave, cologne-ad voice. "*Diabooooolical . . .*"

Everyone grabbed a seat on the couch, eager to see what more would be said.

The reporter, Tiffany, continued, "Here to address this heinous crime spree is the newly elected governor, Diane Foxington."

"Governor?" Wolf gasped, amazed that they'd gotten attention from someone so high up in the government. This was the big time!

On the television screen, a sophisticated-looking fox with a powerful business suit and a "don't-mess-with-me" air about her stepped up to the microphone. Behind her stood the angry-looking police chief. As a gaggle of reporters fired questions at the governor, she held up her hand calmly and said, "We all know how dastardly the Bad Guys are . . ."

Wolf leaned forward, rubbing his hands together. "You *bet* we are!"

"But more than anything," Governor Foxington continued, "I feel sorry for them."

Wolf stared at the screen in horror. "What?!"

The governor continued, "These so-called 'Bad Guys' are really just second-rate has-beens. Behind their amateurish antics and, frankly, *unoriginal* capers, I mean really . . . *another bank* is nothing but a deep well of anger—"

"I ain't angry!" Piranha shrieked. "*You're* angry!" He jumped forward and tried to bite the governor through the TV. Shark gently but firmly pulled him away, so they could see what more she would say.

"—denial," the governor added.

"Not true!" Tarantula snapped.

"—and self-loathing," Diane Foxington continued.

"The only one I self-loathe is *you*!" Snake hissed.

Unable to hear them through the TV, obviously, the governor just rambled on with her ridiculous word vomit. "And those are holes that no amount of cash or priceless art can ever fill."

As she finished her monologue, the Bad Guys all looked uncomfortable. They were used to people fearing them, sure. Hating them, sometimes. Admiring them? Probably. But no one had every pitied and felt bad for them. That was *low*. Wolf wasn't sure what to think about the governor's words. What if some part of what she was saying was . . . *true*?

Snake reached for the remote and asked, "What's on the Food Network?"

But before he could change the channel, the governor had more to get out. "So, let's *forget* about the Bad Guys," she said confidently. "And focus on more positive things! And what could be more positive than the annual Good Samaritan Awards, where tomorrow night I will present the Golden Dolphin to this year's 'Goodest Citizen.'"

Wolf flicked off the TV, fuming. He didn't need to hear any more.

"I can't believe I voted for her," Tarantula muttered.

"You voted for her?" Piranha asked, incredulous.

Tarantula shrugged. "She's good on climate change!"

Snake suddenly noticed that Wolf had a mischievous smile spread across his face. That smile only meant one thing: an idea. A plan. A bad, bad plan. Snake asked, "What—what are you—you've got that *twinkle* in your eye."

Wolf's grin grew even wider. "Guys, who's up for another job?" he asked, his voice a mix of laughter and excitement. "A BIG ONE." He opened one of the shades in the apartment, revealing a giant billboard announcing the "Good Samaritan Awards," with a picture of the famous Golden Dolphin trophy in the center of everything. The dolphin itself was solid gold, with precious emeralds for eyes. It was the ultimate prize, the greatest heist possible in all the world.

"The Golden Dolphin?" Snake asked. "Seriously?"

Piranha was shocked by the idea. "Whoa . . . I thought I was the crazy one."

Snake shook his head. "That job has broken every criminal who's tried it: The Bucharest Bandits, Lucky Jim—"

Piranha cut him off to add another notorious criminal taken down during their quest for the Golden Dolphin, "El Nocturno—"

"The Crimson Paw," Shark piped up.

Tarantula waved one hand. "Hold up! The Crimson Paw was never arrested."

"Yeah," Snake said. "But he never stole anything again after trying and failing to get the Golden Dolphin statue."

Wolf shook his head, undeterred. "Snake, what better way to wipe that smirk off the governor's fuzzy face than stealing the Golden Dolphin from right under her whiskers?" He paused, looking around to try to gauge the rest of the group's opinion. "This is the holy grail of thievery," he pointed out. No one had ever done it before, and there was no reason the Bad Guys couldn't be the first to succeed. "If we pull this off, we will cement our legacy as the greatest criminals of all time!"

Snake wasn't convinced. "Whoa, buddy. I thought we weren't supposed to make things personal! Besides, we've got a good thing going here—friends, freedom . . . and just look at all this loot!" Sure, it could be an amazing heist . . . but what if it all went wrong? They'd lose everything they'd built up until now. Snake didn't want to do this and risk everything, just to prove some politician wrong.

"Alright, you're right." Wolf sighed. "Forget it. The Dolphin job is off. I guess the rodent will get his trophy after all."

"Yeah, I guess he w—" Snake stopped, then swung around

to look at his friend for clarification. "What . . . what do you mean . . . rodent?"

"Oh," Wolf said casually. "Yes, did I not mention that? That's weird, I thought I mentioned that part."

He lifted another curtain, revealing the rest of the billboard outside their secret lair's window. It showed that this year's recipient of the Golden Dolphin award was none other than Professor Marmalade, the cutest—and most delicious-looking—*guinea pig* on Earth!

Shark's giant mouth hung open wide, revealing rows and rows of shiny, sharp teeth. "The Good Samaritan is . . ."

"A *guinea pig*?" Tarantula laughed.

Snake's tongue flicked out of his mouth, tasting air at the mere *thought* of guinea pig. That frozen push pop had done *nothing* to curb his appetite. What he wouldn't give to have a nice, tasty, hairy guinea pig right about now. He snapped backward, but even just looking at the giant image of Professor Marmalade's delicious picture was making him drool.

"Soooo," Wolf said in a singsong voice. "Whadd'ya say, Snakey? *Better than cake*." He grinned; he knew he had Snake right where he wanted him.

Snake growled. "Arrrrgh, okay, *fine*. But he better be delicious."

Everyone else smiled. It was a plan. A big, bad plan. Wolf put his paw into the middle of his group of friends. "Are we all in this together?" he asked, glancing at each of them in turn.

Piranha and Shark both put their fins in. Tarantula put four of her legs in. And finally, Snake put his tail in. It was *on*. "Let's do this!" they all cheered in unison.

Wolf nodded. He couldn't wait. "So here's the plan: Just like every year, the ceremony will be held at the Museum of Fine Arts . . ."

CHAPTER FOUR

The plan was set. They would infiltrate the fancy-pants event at the Museum of Fine Arts, posing as guests who were there to celebrate the life and achievements of that annoying guinea pig, Professor Marmalade. During the festivities, they'd sneak backstage using Webs's clever hacking skills. Wolf finished explaining the plan for the gang, "... where the Golden Dolphin will be positioned just beyond the backstage curtain."

"Pssh," Piranha said, waving a fin. "Sounds easy."

"*Sounds* easy, *hermano*," Wolf agreed. "But to get there, we need to bypass three levels of security. So. Step One: We'll need to blend in."

The Bad Guys all got to work finding their costumes for the night. Since most of their lives were spent stealing, getting gussied up for a party was a new kind of fun. By the time the party rolled around, they were all set. Wolf had chosen a snazzy suit, along with a dapper fedora, silk tie, fake mustache, and tinted glasses. He had mastered the part of fancy movie star, using George Clooney as his muse and guide. That guy always looked good.

Shark, meanwhile, had gone the opposite direction, cramming his body into a gorgeous gown that was stretched to the limit by Shark's massive, muscular form. Perched atop Shark's head, Tarantula had fashioned her long limbs into the shape of a butterfly fascinator hat.

Snake went old-school, complete with a classic suit, handlebar mustache, monocle, top hat, and a pair of fake arms to help fill out the look.

Piranha squeezed into a kid-size coat and tails, looking handsome and a bit childish—but it did the trick.

Every one of them wore a pair of sunglasses to complete the look and to help hide their true identities from anyone who decided to look a little more closely at the characters under the costumes.

When they arrived at the museum, they joined in with a long line of guests who were already milling about, waiting to enter the event. There was a grand staircase stretching up toward the Fine Arts Museum, and the group of disguised Bad Guys had just begun to climb the steps when a stretch limo pulled up at the bottom of the stairs. Many of the guests turned to watch as Professor Marmalade, the eccentric and good-natured do-gooder who would be honored that night, popped out of the limo and began his own march up the stairs to the party. Paparazzi flooded in around the little guinea pig, eager to snap shots of the evening's featured guest.

"Professor Marmalade . . ." Wolf muttered, rolling his eyes. "This year's recipient of the Golden Dolphin and the most annoying good guy on the planet."

Marmalade waved to his crowds of adoring fans, then stepped up to talk with Tiffany Fluffit, the eager news reporter who'd been assigned to the night's festivities. "Professor," Tiffany started. "In the past year, you've stopped wars, fed the hungry, and saved countless pandas." The reporter took a deep breath and flashed a huge smile at the nodding professor. "Some have described your goodness as second only to the Dalai Lama!"

Professor Marmalade nodded, putting on a look of earnest humility. "Oh, Tiffany, it's not a competition! And if it were, it would really be more of a *tie*. But we can all agree that there is a flower of *goodness* inside all of us, just waiting to blossom."

Everyone within earshot broke into applause, overcome with love for the oh-so-good professor. Marmalade waved to the crowd as he continued his climb up the red carpet, heading inside to the awards ceremony where even more fans were waiting for a glimpse of that evening's headliner.

"Once we get inside," Wolf whispered to his friends, "There are two armored doors . . ." He explained how they would get into the doors that were locked and sealed tightly, with extra protections, to ensure that the beloved Golden Dolphin was safe and secure until it was thrust into Professor

Marmalade's grubby little guinea pig paws. "The first door can only be opened by a special key card that is carried at all times by our dear friend, the chief of police," Wolf told the others. "The second is outfitted with a retinal scanner that only works with Governor Foxington's eye, and it's also guarded by an elite special ops unit trained to strike first and ask questions later."

The other Bad Guys nodded.

Wolf pointed out, "Since Governor Foxington is the only one who has clearance to open the second door, Step Two is that she and I will need to get up close and personal . . ."

As soon as they got inside, the Bad Guys searched the room. They had to find the host of the evening's festivities, Governor Diane Foxington, who was busy welcoming guests at the main entrance of the museum. Every so often, she would pose for a picture with an adoring fan, right in front of one of the museum's pieces of art: an abstract sculpture made using rusty, jagged metal beams.

The moment Governor Foxington was alone, having just bid farewell to an ambassador of this or that place, Wolf sidled up beside her. His suit was impeccable, and he fit in perfectly next to the well-dressed governor. "Interesting piece," he said, tipping his chin at the sculpture. "Trashy, pointless, *and* pretentious."

Governor Foxington smiled politely at him. "They say

that art reveals more about the viewer than the artist, Mr. . . . ?" She cocked an eyebrow at him.

Wolf immediately realized he was dealing with a politician who was much smarter than he'd given her credit for. "The name's Poodleton," he said. "Oliver Poodleton." He bent over to kiss her hand, while slyly swiping the diamond ring right off her hand. "You know, it's about time someone stood up to those diabolical Bad Guys. Though I've got to say, no one's succeeded yet."

The governor smirked. "Oh, I don't think it'll be *that* hard."

"I have a feeling it will be harder than you think," Wolf countered. "I'd say they're one epic job away from cementing their legacy."

The governor—*Diane*, Wolf thought, now that he felt they were on a first-name basis—laughed. "Ha! Mr. Poodleton, you're funny!"

"I—I am?" Wolf stammered.

"The only legacy those Bad Guys are cementing is life in prison," Diane said certainly. "Did you see their last job?" She ticked off each of their mistakes on her long fingers. "Unsecured exits, crude disguises, compulsive showboating—I mean, it was a *mess*. All the classic signs of a crew in decline." As her insults continued, Wolf started to feel more and more insecure about his skills as a thief. But then he remembered: *She* didn't know anything. This was just a random politician trying to make people like her.

Diane finished, "Next, they're gonna make it personal. That's when you just *know* the Bad Guys are toast."

Wolf swallowed, trying to hide his discomfort behind a cunning smile. "Uh, well, that's your opinion, *Diane*."

Through a polished smile, she said, "And I'm the governor." She turned to look at the ugly, trash-like sculpture again. "As for the sculpture: I think it's about perspective. If you look closely, even trash can be recycled into something beautiful."

Wolf looked to where she was pointing and noticed that the sculpture's shadow on the wall was in the shape of a gorgeous swan. *Huh.* "How about that?" Wolf mused. "I guess some things aren't always as they appear." Shaking his head to get his confidence back, Wolf tried to jump back to the plan. He grabbed his cell phone, and with the smoothness of cake frosting, he said, "That reminds me . . . may I? I can't miss a photo op with the governor and a pile of garbage!"

"Oh," Diane said, grinning her pearly white polished smile for the camera. "You're too hard on yourself, Mr. Poodleton."

Flash! Wolf snapped the selfie he needed in order to execute the next step of their plan. He'd show that arrogant Governor Foxington just how wrong she was . . . Diane had no idea what was in store for her—and her fancy, schmancy Golden Dolphin—that night!

The Bad Guys were on the move.

CHAPTER FIVE

"Okay, friends," Wolf said, rejoining the others on the far side of the museum's huge entranceway. "It's showtime!" Together, the Bad Guys stepped into the main part of the museum. A big open space had been turned into a reception area for guests of the event. Round banquet tables had been set with multicourse place settings, elegant centerpieces, and at the front of the room was a stage with a podium and a giant screen set up for a video presentation during the award ceremony itself.

"Once we're in," Wolf reminded the guys. "It's on to Step Three: Split up and take our positions."

Nearby, Wolf heard the police chief tell some of her crew, "Officers, if the Bad Guys crash this event, I will definitely lose my job and I will not hesitate to take you down with me. Now move out . . ."

On Wolf's command, the Bad Guys also broke off and moved into position.

Piranha broke away from the others and nonchalantly dove into a nearby fountain to access the building's plumbing system.

Tarantula hopped off Shark's head and crawled stealthily across the floor, in between partygoers' legs and shoes.

Shark sidled up the main staircase, heading for the Ceremony Room and his next move.

Meanwhile, Wolf headed for the balcony level, snagging guests' wallets and jewelry along the way. *Hey, if it's that easy to take,* he reasoned, *the owners* deserve *to lose their stuff to a hard-working thief.*

Downstairs, Snake slithered up a modern art sculpture to reach one of the museum's upper ledges, then slid directly into an air duct.

"Mics on," Tarantula said quietly as soon as she was in position. "Everyone on comms, do you copy?" She hopped onto the back of a security guard, riding undetected as he unlocked the secret surveillance room. Webs was in!

Wolf, Piranha, Snake, and Shark all murmured, "Copy," into their communication devices.

While the rest of the group established their positions, Snake slithered through the air vents. When he'd reached his destination, he paused. In the next moment, he molted out of his skin and costume, leaving both his withered snakeskin and dapper disguise behind. He emerged from the air vent in fresh stealth gear.

Back in the Ceremony Room, Shark was lapping up the life of luxury in his job disguised as a partygoer.

"A drink for a pretty lady?" a waiter asked, leaning in close.

"No thank you," Shark said. "My life is too complicated right now."

Downstairs, Piranha emerged from the water pipes straight into a toilet bowl. Just as he came up from down below, he saw a caterer entering the stall. Unfortunate for the caterer, but fortunate for Piranha. *Attack!* Moments later, wearing the caterer's uniform, Piranha reemerged from the bathroom in a fresh new disguise.

"Boys," Webs whispered into the comm link. "It's dolphin season." Having dispatched with the security guard—by hanging him upside down from the ceiling of the security room with duct tape—Tarantula had successfully hacked into the museum's surveillance system. She could monitor everyone's progress and clearly see everything that was going on in the backstage area. The Golden Dolphin was right where it was supposed to be, sitting backstage waiting for their big moment.

"Copy that," Piranha replied, stepping out of the bathroom in his new caterer's uniform. "I'm on the move."

Back out in the party, Wolf continued to make his rounds. He sauntered past the police chief just as the chief barked, "Unit Two, is the backstage area still secure?"

The response came immediately through the walkie-talkie, "Unit Two, all clear."

"Keep your eyes open, boys," the police chief reminded

them. "They could be anywhere, just waiting to humiliate us."

Just then, Wolf took the opportunity to bump into the chief, who looked up in surprise. "Oh, pardon me, Officer!" Wolf said, placing one hand on her arm.

"Not a problem, sir," the chief said. "I thrive on instinct. This is where all the training pays off . . ."

Without missing a beat, Wolf strode confidently down the hall—with the chief's security key tucked securely in his palm. Slipping it out of her pocket had been *way* too easy.

Keeping her eye on the surveillance videos, Tarantula told the others, "Wolf is in position! Piranha, you penguin-suited and booted?"

Piranha murmured, "Affirmative. I'm a clean, mean, dolphin-stealing machine!" He joined a line of caterers, pushing a cart out toward the event hall space. "What's going on, guys?" he asked some of the other waiters. The key to fitting in, he knew, was to act like you belong. But as soon as no one was looking, Piranha veered off in a different direction and slipped into a janitor's closet.

Security card in hand, Wolf made his way toward a staircase, stealing more wallets and jewelry, making it look as easy as taking candy from a baby. Suddenly, he came upon his easiest mark of the night: a frail and very rich-looking old lady. Dollar bills were spilling out of her purse, and Wolf just couldn't resist. He was on a mission, but a theft like this was impossible to pass up. But just as he grabbed on to the woman's purse strap, the old lady tripped and began to fall down the stairs. The purse strap, held on one side by Wolf, was the only thing keeping her from falling all the way down the stairs.

Wolf glanced at the old lady, then at the purse, then back again. With a quick *heave-ho*, he pulled the old lady back up to safety. He sighed, feeling like a sucker for letting his conscience take over. "Here," he grumbled. "Let me help you. Are you okay, ma'am?"

"Oh my gracious, yes!" she said in a chirpy voice. "I may be dizzy, but I'm alive, thanks to you." She wrapped Wolf in a warm, huge hug.

"Wha—what are you . . . ?" he stammered.

"Oh, thank you, dear," the old lady said, patting him lovingly. "You're such a *good boy*."

As she walked off, Wolf's eyes went wide. His tail had begun to wag uncontrollably. It was a feeling Wolf had never felt before . . . what *was* that? He quickly tucked his tail back into the seat of his pants, making sure no one had seen it slip out of his disguise. A few minutes later, he strolled into the janitor's closet Piranha had set up as a sort of makeshift command station.

"You all good, brother?" Piranha asked, noticing right away that Wolf looked a little off.

"Yeah, yeah. I'm all . . . all good," Wolf told him, trying to shake off his strange encounter with the old lady. Into the radio, he said, "Webs, what do you say about moving on to Step Four?"

Back in the central command post, Webs nodded. "Copy that. Shark, you're up. Do your thing."

Excitedly, Shark blurted out through the radio, "Do I get to improvise?!"

While he climbed into Piranha's catering cart, Wolf muttered back, "Yeah, fine, improvise. But please be subtle."

On the main event floor, Shark was ready to do his thing. His job: distract! So, he hastily spilled his drink, then lifted a table high above his head and hurled it across the room, before beginning to scream like a banshee. "I'm having a BABY! Is there a doctor, or perhaps several SECURITY GUARDS who could LEAVE THEIR POSTS and help me?!"

All nearby security guards quickly abandoned their posts to help out the screaming lady. As soon as they were out of position, Piranha wheeled the catering cart to the door of the guard room. Wolf's hand poked out of the underside of the cart to swipe them in with the stolen key card.

But getting through that first door was the easy part. Now they had to get past two elite special-ops guards keeping watch over the trophy room. Wolf and Piranha surveyed the scene from the far end of the hallway. That's when they noticed a food cart rolling toward the guards. The covered tray on the top of the cart was labeled "Fish Surprise."

"Fish Surprise?" One of the Special Ops guards asked, leaning toward the tray. Curious, he lifted the cover.

"Surprise!" Piranha shouted, leaping into the guards' faces.

That did the trick, and Wolf rushed toward the next part of the plan. He studied the retinal scanner, the last step before they could get through the door. With a flick of his finger, he pulled up the selfie he'd taken with Diane Foxington earlier in the evening. He zoomed in on the governor's face, then hit send. "Webs," he called through his comm device. "You're up."

A nanosecond later, Wolf's phone dinged with an incoming message. "Done!" Webs chirped back. "Eight steps ahead of ya, Wolfie."

Wolf looked at the photo message. Tarantula had zoomed in and enhanced the picture to get a high-res image of Diane's iris. Wolf pressed his phone up against the retinal scanner, watching as the light blinked green.

They were in. The heist was ON.

CHAPTER SIX

"Ladies and gentlemen," an announcer called out to all the distinguished guests who'd gathered together for the main event. "Introducing your emcee for the Good Samaritan Awards . . . president of the committee, Governor Diane Foxington!"

As everyone clapped, Shark continued to keep the guards occupied at the back of the room. But as soon as Wolf muttered into the comm unit that they were in, Shark patted his dress and took a deep breath. "False alarm, guys! I forgot . . . I'm not pregnant."

Back at the front of the room, Diane walked to the podium. "Thank you, thank you so much." She solemnly addressed the crowd while footage of the most horrific natural disaster in the history of the city played on the screen behind her. "Last year," she reminded the partygoers, "we faced our biggest test when a meteorite crashed into our dear city." On the screen, a massive meteor flew through the sky and landed smack dab in the middle of LA. "That meteorite didn't just make a hole in our city," Diane said, her voice serious. "It made a hole in our hearts."

On-screen behind her there was a video of people gathered at the edge of the smoldering crater, crying into the debris. "But even in tragedy," Diane went on, "Professor Marmalade did what he does so well . . ." The screen switched to footage of the night's hero, the tiny guinea pig, making his shocking discovery: that the meteorite looked like a massive heart. "He made us look at things differently. Where we saw a catastrophe, he saw a heart. In our city's darkest moment, Professor Marmalade lifted our spirits and brought hope back to all of us!"

Everyone in the audience—and on-screen—cheered for their city's hero: the good-hearted Professor Marmalade.

"Thanks to Marmalade," Diane finished, "'The 'Love Crater Meteorite' will forever serve as a reminder that there is goodness, even in the worst places."

The governor's presentation was moving, to be sure, but the Bad Guys had better things to do. Now that they'd easily nipped past all the security, it was time to get what they'd come for, and get out. Wolf and Piranha ripped off their tuxedos, revealing the full-body tactical suits they were wearing underneath. They launched themselves over the gauntlet of laser beams surrounding the Golden Dolphin trophy. As they flew through the air, a vent in the ceiling popped open and Snake popped out—just in time to catch his two pals zipping through the air. "Need a lift?" Snake said seriously.

Wolf, Snake, and Piranha all dangled directly above the Golden Dolphin. Success was so close, Snake could almost *smell* it with his tongue when he flicked it out to say, "Hurry up!"

They sunk lower and lower, getting closer and closer to the trophy. "This is going surprisingly smoothly," Wolf mused. But just as he said that, the diamond ring he'd slipped off Governor Foxington's hand earlier in the night fell out of a pocket in his tactical suit. It bounced on the Golden Dolphin, then pinged back up into the air. Wolf grabbed it with the tip of his shoes, but it was too late—dozens of laser cannons flipped out of the base of the Golden Dolphin pedestal and fired into the air.

Pew!

Pew!

Pew!

Wolf's shoes were scorched to black, and when the laser hit a nearby statue, the whole thing was vaporized.

"What the molt just happened?" Snake gasped.

Wolf used his superior wolf vision to read the plaque on the front of the trophy stand. "The Golden Dolphin is protected by the . . ." he paused. "The Wolf/Piranha/Snake/Shark/Tarantula Protection System!"

Over the radio, Webs gasped. "The WPSST?"

The laser cannons were motion sensitive, carefully

tracking even the slightest movement. Wolf, Snake, and Piranha appeared to be trapped. "This was not supposed to happen!" Wolf wailed.

"You think?!" Snake snapped back.

"Calm down," Webs told them both. "I'm on it." She inserted a USB drive into the museum's main system. "Initiating WPSST *override protocol*." She laughed confidently to herself. This was beginner's stuff. "Get it, queen!"

Instantaneously, a DENIED message flashed on-screen.

"Did it work?" Wolf asked over the comm device.

Tarantula tapped at a few keys, muttering, "Give me five minutes!"

"We don't *have* five minutes!" Snake snarled.

Back in the main auditorium, Diane had finished her presentation and was moving on to the main event. "Please join me in welcoming to the stage, this year's distinguished honoree . . . Professor Marmalade!"

The guinea pig strolled out onstage, bowing as guests offered him a standing ovation and loud cheers from all corners of the room. "We love you, Professor Marmalade!" one attendee screamed out, sounding like a fan at a rock concert.

"The pig is on the move," Shark whispered into his comm unit, doing his part of the mission—keeping watch over the festivities. "I repeat, the pig is on the move!"

"*Vamonos*," Piranha said, sounding desperate. "We gotta go!"

"Webs!" Wolf cried, from where he was still hanging over the spot where the Golden Dolphin statue used to be. "Webs! The curtain's going up any minute." She had to get them out of there!

Tarantula was working as fast as she could. But just when she thought she almost had things cracked, there was a knock on the door of the Security Room. Webs turned and gasped—she had company!

"Hey, Larry!" The police chief's voice echoed through the thick door. "Open up. What did we say about locking doors?"

With a quick glance at the still-locked door, Tarantula whispered into her comm unit, "Shark, I got a situation here."

"Copy that," Shark said, heading out of the party. "I'm on my way."

"It's not letting me in," Tarantula growled, half to herself and half to her teammates, as she kept trying to hack into the system to override the lasers that were still circling Wolf, Piranha, and Snake.

"Did you try rebooting?" Wolf asked.

"You probably need to download a driver," Snake suggested helpfully.

"Check your system preferences," Wolf added.

"Oh my gosh!" Tarantula gasped. "You guys fixed it!"

"Really?" Wolf and Snake both asked at the same time.

"NO!" Tarantula snapped back. As if she hadn't tried *all* those things already. She was the team *hacker*, after all. "It's time to turn this baby on beast mode!"

Pop!

Pop!

Pop!

Three new keyboards suddenly appeared out of Webs's main terminal. Now she could get more hands on the job. "Eat *that*, WPSST!" Her eight legs went immediately into overdrive on all her keyboards. She quickly started unlocking each of the WPSST's security firewalls at an unbelievable speed.

From outside, the chief pounded on the door again. "I'm starting to get mad here, Larry!"

Tarantula was working as fast as possible, but she knew she didn't have much time left. As if to confirm her fears, Piranha suddenly squeaked through the comm unit, "Hurry up, guys!" A moment later, he briefly lost his grip on the other two, which made Snake and Wolf slip down just the slightest bit. Panic-stricken, Piranha released a giant fart straight into the air duct they were dangling from. "No no no no no!" he groaned.

But it was too late for regrets. The fart was out, and now it was traveling through the museum's system of duct work. The odor slipped into the Security Room, and Webs got a whiff immediately. "Piranha! Are you *kidding* me?" The air was quickly filled with the power of Piranha's powerful gas. Webs knew she had to work even quicker now before she suffocated or lost consciousness.

"Sorry," Piranha whined, his voice carrying through the vents.

The chief pounded on the door again. "Is this because I ate your leftovers?"

Webs held her breath and glanced at the door. There wasn't much time left. Through the surveillance system, she could hear Professor Marmalade onstage, saying, ". . . and that's why, at my Gala for Goodness, we will raise all the money needed . . ."

Tarantula could barely see through the cloud of toxic fart. But she continued to work furiously, so they could finish their mission and *get out*. Outside the door, she could hear the police chief rattling a set of keys. *No*, Webs thought, *she can't have another key, can she?*

Onstage, Governor Foxington was saying, "And now, the moment we've all been waiting for . . ."

That's when Tarantula lost consciousness. Which was *extra* unfortunate timing since it was *also* at that moment that the chief of police slid her spare key into the lock and opened the door to the security room. But before she could get a good look at the scene before her, there was a tap on the chief's shoulder.

"Excuse me," Shark said, composed and full of charm. "Is this the LADIES room?"

"What?" the chief said, momentarily startled. "Huh?"

With the door to the Security Room now open, the fart fumes cleared. Tarantula woke up, shook her head to clear it, and immediately got back to work. With not a second to spare, she cracked the WPSST code!

Onstage, Governor Foxington opened the curtain around the Golden Dolphin—but there was nothing there!

No Golden Dolphin.

No Bad Guys.

Nothing.

"No!" Diane screamed, immediately realizing what had happened. But moments later, she regained her composure and tried to calm the panic-stricken crowd. "Everyone! Everyone! Please don't panic. Just stay calm!" She held up her hands, attempting to silence the room. "I'm sure there's an explanation for this. I repeat. Please do NOT panic."

Using the chaos around them as a cover, the Bad Guys quickly changed back into their partygoer disguises and discreetly made their way past the screaming crowd, creeping toward the front door. "Nice work," Wolf told them. "Now, let's make like a wolf and get the pack out of here."

"Ah, wordplay," Piranha said, chuckling. Then, after a quick pause, he added, "Wait, I don't get it."

Onstage, Marmalade stepped up to the mic. "Diane, Diane, if I may." The crowd calmed slightly at the sight of their composed guest of honor coming forward to speak. "You have to understand. I didn't create the love crater and bring hope back to the city for an award . . ." Everyone's focus was now on Marmalade. The Bad Guys were almost home free, out the door, when Marmalade added, "I did these good things because of how they made me feel . . . that tingly feeling . . . the shiver up my spine . . . that *wag* in my tiny tail!"

When Marmalade said those final words, Wolf stilled. He remembered that feeling, from when he'd helped that old lady earlier in the night! He paused, unable to resist the pull to find out what the pig would say next.

"Because you see . . . being good, just *feels* so good. And when you're good, you're *loved*."

Wolf's tail began to wag. While he scrambled to hide it, his glasses and fake mustache slipped off. Seeing what was happening, Snake called out, "Wolf? Wolf!"

"What are you doing?" Piranha screeched.

"Go!" Shark and Webs both hollered. "Go!"

But Wolf was transfixed. The idea of having that wag in his tail all the time, of being *loved* . . . it was as though Professor Marmalade was speaking his language!

Suddenly, someone in the audience screamed: "IT'S THE BAD GUYS!"

"Arrest them!" The chief of police called out, pointing right to where Wolf and his crew were standing. "Arrest them before they get away!"

The Bad Guys froze as hundreds of guards surrounded them, ready with their batons. They were trapped, and there appeared to be no escape.

"They stole the Golden Dolphin!" the police chief growled, staring down each of the Bad Guys in turn.

"Come on," Wolf snapped, finally snapping out of the trance Professor Marmalade's little speech had trapped him in. "You can't prove that."

Just then, the Golden Dolphin slipped out the bottom of Shark's dress and clanked to the ground. Shark looked down at the trophy, then up at the cops, then back down at the prize. "My—my—my baby!"

The police closed in on them, eager to keep the Bad Guys contained. They knew all too well just how easily the Bad Guys could slip out of a tight spot. "On your knees, Bad Guys, with your hands up!" the police chief ordered.

"Never," Snake hissed. "We're out of here."

"So long, suckers!" Wolf added, grabbing the grappling hook gun he'd anchored to his pants. He shot it toward the ceiling, smirking about their clever escape plan. But instead of carrying the guys up and to safety, the cable snagged the back of Wolf's pants . . . and carried his pants up and away, leaving him mostly naked down below.

Wolf's grin slipped, and he covered his undies with his hands. "Well," he said awkwardly. "This just got weird."

CHAPTER SEVEN

BAD GUYS LOSE FREEDOM & PANTS IN DOLPHIN DEBACLE

"The bad guys go bust!" Tiffany Fluffit reported as she and her news crew stood at the front of the art museum. The cameras were rolling as the Bad Guys were dragged from the gaping front entrance, handcuffed and struggling. "The nefarious fivesome has finally been captured. I, Tiffany Fluffit, am first on the scene!"

As she tugged Wolf toward the police van, the police chief was euphoric. "Wow," she said, unable to contain her excitement. "I just realized that I have devoted my entire adult life to putting you in jail. You are my purpose. Without you, who am I?" She shook her head, laughing. "Ha! Just kiddin'. This is the best moment of my life! It's the end of the Bad Guys! Alright, your chariot awaits."

While the news crew carried on filming, the police loaded the Bad Guys into a heavily armored police wagon.

"No! Get off me!" Tarantula griped. "You're begging for a biting right now!"

Piranha snapped his jaws at his captor. "Take your hands offa me!"

Snake cried out, "Wolf!" just before he, too, was thrown in the wagon. This was *exactly* what Snake had been afraid would happen. This heist was too personal, too risky, and they got caught. But when he locked eyes with his bud, he could tell Wolf's gears were turning. It looked like he had something up his sleeve . . .

Just then, Governor Foxington and Professor Marmalade exited the museum, watching as the Bad Guys were tossed into the back of the police van. Reporters called out to them, eager for their take on the evening's events. "Professor Marmalade! Madame Governor!"

"One at a time . . ." Diane said, holding up a hand for calm.

But before the first reporter could pose a question, Wolf's voice cut through the din. "Excuse me!" he called out. "Sorry to interrupt. I just wanted to congratulate the governor here. Gotta say, you really had us pegged. We're just a deep well of anger, self-loathing . . ."

"Denial—" Diane added to the list of criticisms.

"Sure," Wolf said, cutting her off.

"Narcissism, emotional emptiness—" she blurted.

Wolf broke in again, "So we're on the same page." She could stop talking now.

We're the Bad Guys!

I'm the charismatic leader. (This is Wolf, by the way!) Shark is the master of disguise. Tarantula is the ultimate hacker. Snake is our resident safecracker. And Piranha, well, he's the muscle.

Don't get me wrong, we've all been known to don a disguise or two. We look pretty dashing, don't we?

It doesn't always get us out of trouble . . .

Especially when that do-gooder Professor Marmalade and Governor Foxington are involved.

Sometimes we may get into sticky situations. And by that, I mean drowning in thousands of mind-controlled guinea pigs.

But what really matters is sticking together even when the odds are stacked against us.

We're just trying to be good after all. I promise.

Snake glanced at the other guys, who were all piled up in the police wagon. "Where's he going with this?" he muttered.

"Sadly," Wolf continued. "We were never given a chance to be anything more than second-rate criminals. If only there was someone who could help the *flower of goodness inside us* blossom? Some icon of love and forgiveness, like, I dunno . . ." He coughed, then winked at Professor Marmalade. "Someone like the Dalai Lama." With a sigh, Wolf added, "Best thing is to just throw us in jail for the rest of our hopeless lives—"

"That's the plan," the police chief agreed in a chipper voice. "And it makes me smile just thinking about it!" She stepped forward to shove Wolf into the wagon with the rest of the crew.

But Wolf wasn't about to give up just yet. His plan would work, he was sure of it. And then, just like that, things clicked into place. "Wait!" Marmalade called out. "Stop!"

Bingo! Wolf thought, trying to hide his smile.

The professor sashayed down a few of the museum's steps, making his way toward the police wagon. "Mr. Wolf may be a savage beast," he said. "Basically walking garbage—" He cut himself off, turning to Wolf, and said, "Sorry. I'm making a point."

Wolf shrugged. "Do what you need to do, pal."

"But how can we say they're hopeless," Marmalade

asked, performing for the group of people and reporters who had gathered around, "if they've never been given a chance?"

There was a din of conversation, as everyone tried to figure out what he was talking about.

Marmalade held up his hands, urging patience from the crowd. "What if we tried a little experiment, Diane? As you know, my Gala for Goodness, the—hashtag—*charity event of the year*, is coming up. If I can prove to everyone at the gala that the Bad Guys have changed, will you set them free and give them a clean start?"

The crowd gasped. Before the governor could reply, the police chief rushed over. "What?? No! No no no. Professor, don't you see what he's doing? He's playing you."

"But it was my idea!" Marmalade argued.

"It *was* his idea," Wolf agreed, grinning.

"Only because you pushed the idea on him!" the police chief sputtered at Wolf.

Everyone watched to see what the governor's response would be. Finally, she held up a finger and said her piece. "Professor, I am not about to put the safety of the city on the line for an experiment."

Wolf broke in, his voice like silk. "Excuse me, Madame Governor, I seem to remember that a wise person once said 'Even trash can be recycled into something beautiful.'"

Diane considered this. "Okay," she said eventually. "I'm game . . ."

The police chief was horrified. "No!"

"But," Diane added, "we'll hold on to the Dolphin until the gala . . . just to remove any unnecessary temptation."

"Of course!" Professor Marmalade agreed. "Good thinking. That's why you're governor!" The tiny rodent passed the Golden Dolphin to the chief as Wolf's eyes tracked its course. "Now that everyone's happy . . ."

"Grrr!" The police chief said, stamping a foot. "I'm! Not! Happy!"

The little guinea pig beamed for the crowd. "I, Rupert Marmalade the Fourth, will turn the Bad Guys into . . . THE GOOD GUYS!" The crowd erupted in cheers, engulfing Professor Marmalade as soon as he'd uttered those magic words.

Behind him, Wolf slipped out of his cuffs, then stepped into the police van a free man. "I think these belong to you," he said, handing them back to the police chief. Then he tipped his head in Diane's direction and winked.

Diane winked back. "Not everyone gets a second chance. Make the most of it. *Mr. Poodleton.*"

Inside the police wagon, the rest of the gang stared in bewilderment at Wolf. They were confused and angry, wondering what on Earth he'd just done, what kind of bargain he'd gotten them roped into. "Uh, Wolf?" Snake snapped. "What are you doing?"

"What?" Wolf asked nonchalantly. Everyone stared at him, waiting for a real answer. "Oh, *that*! I'm sorry, I thought it was obvious." He paused, then added, "We're going to go good."

"Uh . . ." Tarantula gaped at him. "You totally lost me."

"I told him to stop drinking out of the toilet," Piranha said, shaking his head.

"Hey . . ." Shark said, sounding worried. "Did you get hit on the head?"

Wolf shook his head. "No, I didn't get hit on the head."

"My cousin got hit on the head with an anchor and after that, he only swam in a circle," Shark said, sinking lower at the memory of his cousin.

"No, no," Wolf said. "Guys, guys, guys. You're not following me. We are going to *pretend* to go good."

Everyone stared blankly at Wolf.

"Just a few days with Marmalade . . ." Wolf explained patiently. "Talking about our feelings, drinking cucumber water, 'I'm so sorry, I'll never be a cool criminal again,' yadda yadda yadda—and *then*, we roll into the gala as the Good Guys, and roll out scot-free with . . ."

"The Golden Dolphin!" the other four exclaimed at once.

Wolf nodded. *Now* it was making sense. "You got it. Since

when do we not finish a job? The *Bad* Guys become the *Good* Guys, so we can stay the Bad Guys. You know what I'm saying?"

Snake grinned. This was good. *Sssso* good. "Bad guys acting good! It's the ultimate Bad Guy thing. It's FANTASTIC! Wolf, you're a genius!" He paused for a second, realizing something. "Wait . . . what do we know about being good?"

"C'mon." Wolf shrugged. "It's easy peasy. I mean, you know. How hard can it be? This is going to be the most relaxing con ever. Like a vacation."

They all laughed as their police wagon drove them off to Marmalade's mansion and the next step in their ultimate plan.

Shark chuckled and added, "A con-cation!"

CHAPTER EIGHT

Professor Marmalade's mansion was stunning, a gorgeous and majestic compound in sunny Malibu. Wolf's secret lair was great and all, but this compound was a whole new level of elegance. "Now we're talking!" Piranha cheered as the police van pulled into the professor's massive drive.

"Wow! Big and fancy!" Tarantula said.

Shark stared in awe. "Rodent's got taste!"

"Almost makes me wanna be cute," Snake grumbled.

As the Bad Guys stepped past the front door, Marmalade's voice echoed out all around them, "They say experience is the best teacher. And they are wrong. I am."

Inside, Marmalade was waiting for them, nestled inside the giant, loving hands of his eager manservant, Cuddles. "Good morning, students of goodness, and welcome to the first day of the rest of your *best* life."

Piranha, who'd been taking in the whole scene, suddenly giggled and pointed. "A giant butt!" The others turned to see what he was referring to. It was a marble replica of the Love Crater Meteorite (which did—in fact—look somewhat butt-*like* . . . even if most people preferred to say it looked like a heart) held up by a tiny marble Professor Marmalade sculpture.

"It's not a butt!" Marmalade snapped. "It's a *lamp* in the shape of the Love Crater Meteorite, my greatest good deed." He clapped, turning the lamp on and off, to demonstrate how it worked.

"I wonder whose butt it is," Piranha muttered.

"Once again," Marmalade growled, "it's not a butt, thank you. It's a heart. Now, as I was saying . . ."

"Then why does it have cheeks?" Piranha blurted. "I've never seen a lamp with cheeks."

Shark tried to shush Piranha; this was not the best way to get off to a good start with their host. Their job was to get Marmalade to trust them and like them, so they could trick him!

"It's not a—" Marmalade began once more.

Piranha giggled and yelled out, "BOOOOO-TAY!!"

Marmalade exploded. "IT IS NOT A BUTT!"

The Bad Guys froze. This guy obviously had a *temper*.

Under his breath, Piranha muttered, "Does he even know what a butt is?"

"As I was saying!" Marmalade continued, frustrated. "On the outside, the five of you are villains, predators, remorseless sociopaths—"

"Oh, stop, you're making me blush." Shark fanned himself, honored by the compliments. It felt so good to be bad.

Marmalade glared at him. "But inside, there's a flower! The flower of goodness. And when it blooms—and you feel that tingle of positivity radiating through your body—you're going to want to feel it all the time! But not just any tingle . . . the tingle of goodness." As Wolf tried to hide his tail, which had—once again—begun to wag, Marmalade led them through his house. "You'll find this tingle of goodness in my state-of-the-art Sharing Laboratory."

Wolf tried to hide a laugh. This guy was too much!

Marmalade continued, "Okay, Mr. Snake, I'm going to give you a push pop."

Snake's mouth began to water at the sight of his favorite tasty snack.

He licked his lips and lunged. "Great!" he cheered. "Push pop, just for me!"

But Marmalade pulled the push pop out of the way and explained, "No, to share."

"Why?" Snake asked, his belly humming with excitement.

Marmalade feigned patience. "Well, on a fundamental level, it's about putting someone else's needs ahead of your own."

Shark smiled and nodded, waiting. This time, his buddy

had no *choice* but to give him the push pop! It was part of the exercise. Part of their plan.

"Oh no!" Snake snapped. "No way!"

Wolf warned, "Snake . . ."

"Ugh," Snake grumbled. "Alright, alright."

Shark grinned. "This is gonna taste extra sweet," he told Snake. "'Cause I know how baaad you want it." Snake reluctantly extended the push pop toward Shark. "Pop me, please!" Shark said, smiling more.

"Nope!" Snake said. "Sucker!" Then he quickly swallowed down the push pop in one quick gulp.

"That's it!" Shark fumed. "I'll teach you to share!" He opened his mouth and swallowed *Snake* in one quick gulp. Ha! Now he had taught Snake a lesson *and* the push pop was in *his* belly! "I like sharing! It's yummy!"

Marmalade watched the "sharing" action unfold with a horrified expression on his face. "Well, that's terrifying. Let's try something simpler." As soon as Shark had spit Snake out again, the professor led the gang poolside, and brought them to the base of a tall tree. Overhead, a stranded cat meowed helplessly.

"Hey, look!" Wolf said, pointing. "It's a cat stuck in a tree!"

Marmalade nodded. "It doesn't get much simpler than that. Now, what in this scenario would give you that *good* tingle?"

"Eating it," Snake blurted. "This is why I always carry two pieces of bread with me." He held up two slices of sandwich bread.

"No, I want you to s-s-s-s—" Marmalade prompted.

"Skin it?" Snake guessed.

"Stab it?" Shark tried.

Piranha said, "Sing to it?"

Webs asked, "Saute it?"

Overhead, the cat's eyes went wide. "Meowwwww . . ."

Marmalade sighed. "SAVE it. I want you to *save* it."

The Bad Guys all nodded. "Ohhhh. Right, right, right." They turned to the tree, and took turns snarling out, in increasingly terrifying voices, "HERE, KITTY KITTY! HERE!"

The cat freaked out. She had *zero* interest in being "saved" by any of these wannabe "good guys." She climbed higher up into the tree, trying to add even more space between herself and the ground and her so-called helpers.

"Whoa," Snake said. "The cat is obviously defective."

"What is wrong with you?!" Piranha asked his pals. "You're gonna give it a heart attack. I'll handle this . . ." A second later, Piranha rocketed himself up to the top of the tree. "WHAT'S UP, PAPA?!!" Piranha screamed at the cat.

Now in total freak-out mode, the cat tumbled out of the tree—trying to get away from Piranha. She landed directly on

Wolf, ripping his fur to shreds with her claws. "Aaaahhh! Get him off my face! He's on my face!" Wolf screeched. "Get it off, get it off, get it off!"

"No! No no no!" Marmalade screamed. "What are you doing?"

Marmalade's servant, Cuddles, stepped forward to take the cat. The cat squirmed, then raced back up the tree. Stuck-in-a-tree was better than stuck-with-these-guys, any day.

Marmalade sighed. "What, may I ask, *are* you good at?"

"Uh, stealing stuff?" Piranha suggested.

The other guys chimed in, "Yeah! We're great at that."

"Extortion, robbery—" Snake added.

"Larceny—" said Webs.

"Wire fraud," Piranha put in.

"Tax evasion," Wolf reminded them.

Shark piped up, "Heists—"

"Mail fraud—" Webs went on.

"Wait!" Marmalade said, cutting them off. "Heists, you say?"

"Well, yeah." Wolf nodded. "It's kind of our specialty."

Marmalade's tiny mouth curled into a smile. "I might just have an idea."

CHAPTER NINE

That afternoon, Professor Marmalade and Cuddles led the Bad Guys to a bright, fancy-looking science lab. Protesters were gathered outside the building, holding signs that read, "Free the Guinea Pigs!" The group could hear the protesters chanting that same refrain, over and over, near the front doors of the facility.

"This is an animal testing lab," the professor explained. "Within, 200,000 helpless guinea pigs, all being poked and prodded by sadistic scientists."

Snake began to drool. "Guinea pigs, you say?"

"When you use your criminal skills to rescue my fluffy brethren," Marmalade told them, "there is no way you won't tingle. You might even *wag*."

In a trancelike state, Snake muttered again, "Guinea pigs, you say . . ."

"Snaaaake!" Wolf warned.

Marmalade held out a tiny hand, asking for patience. "I want you to rescue them. But this is a heist for *good*. So, I brought something more . . . friendly for you to wear."

He joyfully presented the Bad Guys with a set of cute animal onesies for them to use as disguises. Wolf would be working this job dressed as a sheep, Snake as a unicorn, Piranha as a fluffy teddy bear, Shark as a harmless walrus, and Tarantula as a foolish lemur. It was the ultimate humiliation. "I'll meet you at the front gate in fifteen minutes. Bye-ee!" He sped off, leaving the guys alone for the first time all day.

Tarantula glanced down at his lemur suit. "Is he serious?"

Piranha shrugged, snuggling into his teddy bear suit. "At least it's comfy."

Wolf gathered the gang together to lay out his plan. He pointed to a window on the second floor of the lab, where a scientist was working away. "That's our way in," he told the others. "We need to distract those scientists." He nodded at Shark. "Shark, you're up."

"Copy that," Shark agreed.

Still outside, the other guys began working on *their* part of the plan. "We're gonna need a rope to get up there," Wolf said. "And a hook."

Snake said, "I got this one!"

The rest of the guys looked at Snake, immediately suspicious. "You're *volunteering*?" Piranha asked.

"You've never volunteered for *anything*," Wolf reminded him. "Ever."

"Sure I did. Right now. Throw me up there!!" Snake hollered. "Giddyup!"

"Really?" Wolf asked, pointing to the window.

"Yup!" Snake said. "Let's do it! ROPE ME!"

By that point, Shark had snuck inside the lab and was now wearing a fake mustache and carrying a baseball mitt. "Hey there, son," he said to the scientist working inside the lab.

"D-d-dad?" the scientist stammered.

Shark nodded. "I know you've got an important job, but I hope you still have time for catch with your old man."

"Oh!" the scientist said, shocked.

"You'll always be my special boy!" Shark cooed.

The scientist raced toward the door. "I've been waiting my entire life for this moment!"

"Okay, then," Shark said, grinning as he held up a baseball. "Now, go long!"

As soon as the scientist was gone, Shark thrust his fin out the window and caught Snake. The rest of the team used Snake's body to crawl up and into the window.

Once they were inside, the guys regrouped outside the lab's steel door, which led into the guinea pig testing area. "All right," Marmalade said, his voice cracking over the radio. "The only way in is through the vents."

Snake was already climbing into the vent. "I got it! Upsy-daisy!"

Wolf glared as Snake's tail disappeared into the vent. He could tell his buddy was up to something . . . something decidedly *not* good.

"I've never seen him so chipper," Shark noted. "Has he been meditating?"

As he slithered through the vents, Snake felt good. *Sooooo* good. Heading toward the testing area full of guinea pigs, he sang, "*Over the filters and through the vents, to guinea pig land we go . . .*" He sniffed and licked the air, working his way closer and closer to the little rodents. Suddenly, he fell from a vent, down, down into a dark room.

It took a moment for his eyes to adjust to the darkness, but when they did, Snake could hardly believe what he was seeing: It was a whole room packed *full* of his very favorite snack. And he had the whole place all to himself! "Snake attack . . ." he muttered.

"Come on, Snake!" Wolf called, a few minutes later. "Snake, open up."

Eventually, the door to the central vault swung open. "Relax," Snake told him. "These doors are complicated. Takes a lot of finesse."

But as soon as the other Bad Guys made their way into the guinea pig vault, they could see *exactly* what had taken so long. Snake's belly was *full* of guinea pigs. He was loaded down like Santa Claus with his bag of presents—but

Snake's bag was his *belly*, and his presents were *guinea pigs*!

"Are you kidding me?!" the rest of the Bad Guys shrieked.

"What do you think you're doing?" Wolf growled. "We're supposed to save them, not eat them!"

Snake licked his lips. "Well, I'd say they've gone to a better place." He burped, tasting the smell of rodent on the air once more.

"Alright," Wolf grumbled. "That's it." He picked Snake up and began to swing him around like a lasso. Guinea pigs began to fly everywhere, spewing out of Snake's belly like gunfire. "Spit! Them! Out!" As they shot across the room, the guinea pigs squealed and scattered, trying desperately to escape while Shark, Piranha, and Tarantula tried to wrangle them. "Calm down!" Wolf ordered. "We're saving you, you stupid hairballs."

Outside the lab, Marmalade's limo pulled up to the front of the testing facility. He greeted the protesters, who were still gathered outside. "Hey, look!" one of the protesters shouted. "It's Professor Marmalade! He's here to save the guinea pigs!"

Marmalade bowed and waved. "Yes, that's right. Help has arrived!"

The protesters all held up cameras, eager to capture the moment of their hero's triumph.

"Keep watching," Marmalade told them all. "Any second now . . ."

Just then, another guinea pig flew out of Snake's mouth and—*bing!*—hit the latch on the doors to the facility. The pressure from the crush of terrified guinea pigs trying to make their escape caused the doors to fling open. The guinea pigs stampeded out of the building, squealing in terror, as the Bad Guys chased after them. Wolf set Snake down, mid-spin.

"It's not what it looks like," Wolf said to Marmalade and the protesters. Though even *Wolf* could see this whole scene really didn't look good.

And then, moments later, Snake coughed, and the final guinea pig popped out of his mouth. The protestors all gasped, horrified to see what exactly had been going on inside the lab during the Bad Guys' supposed rescue mission.

Standing before the crowd, Marmalade slowly shook his head. It was becoming clear this plan to turn the Bad Guys *good* was going to be a whole lot more complicated than he'd bargained for.

CHAPTER TEN

The next day, Governor Diane Foxington paced in front of the Bad Guys, inside Marmalade's mansion. She held up a newspaper with a frozen image of the Bad Guys splashed across the cover. The headline read: "BAD GUYS TERRORIZE ADORABLE RODENTS." She glared at the crew, who were all smart enough to pretend to look sheepish.

"Trespassing! Mayhem! Assault with a deadly reptile!" She ticked off their crimes as she scolded them for the previous evening's events. "As if those poor rodents haven't been through enough already! I'm sorry, Professor, but this experiment is over. I'm calling the chief." She pulled out her phone and marched out of the room.

Marmalade trailed after her, begging, "Experiments take time . . ."

"You couldn't help yourself," Wolf growled at Snake as soon as they'd left. His pal had ruined it for all of them, with his air-tasting, guinea-pig obsessed ways.

"So I had a moment of weakness," Snake argued. "Sue me!"

"That's going to be difficult to do from prison!" Wolf snapped.

"Guys." Webs sighed. "What do we do now?"

Wolf said, "It's time to launch a charm offensive." He put on his biggest smile.

"Oh yeah," Shark said, nodding. "The *Full Clooney*."

Wolf chased after Marmalade and Diane, who were now chatting in the atrium. He got there just as Marmalade said, ". . . you don't understand, they were *trying* to rescue them—"

Wolf cut him off. "Let me talk to Diane," he said, oozing charm. "I got this."

Marmalade stepped back, letting Wolf do his thing.

"Madame Governor," he said, his voice smooth and flirty. "Diane!"

Diane lifted an eyebrow. "Do *not* try to Clooney me, Wolf."

Wolf wasn't deterred. "Oh, I see what's going on. You think I'm still a Bad Guy! Just trying to bamboozle my way to freedom. But we've changed. That flower of goodness? It's blossoming all over the place."

Diane glared at him, exasperated. "Don't you ever get tired of lying?"

"No," Wolf said quickly. Then, "I mean—fudge, that's a trick question, isn't it?"

"I gave you an opportunity!" Diane blurted out. "A chance to show the world that you're more than just a scary stereotype. But you're too proud, or too gutless, to take advantage of it!"

Wolf cringed. "Gutless? *I'm* gutless? I'm sorry, have we met? I'm the villain of every story! Guilty until proven innocent. Even if, by some miracle, we *did* change—who's gonna believe us? Of course, you wouldn't know anything about that, with your Little Miss Perfect power suits."

"Miss Perfect, huh?" Diane spat back. "Is that so?" She pulled out the diamond ring Wolf stole from her during the museum heist.

Wolf patted his pocket, where he'd been sure the ring was still nestled, safe and sound. "Wait a second . . . what?" Had she *stolen* it back? Diane flicked the ring at him, and he caught it. "How did you . . . ?"

Diane rolled her eyes. "A wolf and a fox are not so different," she said. "Maybe they will believe you, maybe they won't. But it doesn't matter. Don't do it for them—do it for *you*. This is a chance to write your own story. To find a better life for you *and* your friends! Come on, what have you got to lose?"

"I dunno." Wolf shrugged. Then he lifted one fluffy eyebrow and suggested, "My dignity?"

Diane eyed up the footie pajamas he was still wearing from

the heist. "Yeah, well, that ship has already sailed." She pocketed her phone, then stepped outside and into her car. She rolled down the driver's side window. "Believe it or not, I'm rooting for you, Wolf."

"So, you're not going to call the chief?" Wolf asked.

She didn't answer. "I'll see you at the gala?" Then she drove off, leaving Wolf to think about all the things she'd said. Was it time for him to drop the act? Could it be time for the Bad Guys to drop the *act* of being good . . . and actually try to *be* good?

Later that night, while the other guys relaxed inside the mansion, Wolf wandered out to sit under the tree with the trapped cat. With Diane's words from that afternoon still ringing in his ears, he was ready to try this again. This time, instead of trying to lure the cat down from the tree, Wolf climbed up. The cat meowed in terror, but Wolf hushed her. "Shhh." He continued to climb until he was an arm's length away from the frightened cat. "Hey there, kitty. I think we got off to a bad start. The name's Wolf."

The cat stepped backward, cowering.

"Yeah," Wolf said sadly. "I get that a lot. First impressions and all. Story of my life."

Suddenly, the cat slipped off her branch. Wolf instinctively reached out and caught her, setting the poor kitty gently on a more stable branch. Then he backed away, giving the cat some space. "It's okay," he promised. "I'm not going to hurt you. I know you're scared. I would be, too, if I were you. But you don't have to be. Just gimme a chance. Truth is, we actually have a lot in common."

The cat looked at him warily.

Wolf leaned a little closer and whispered, "Don't tell anyone, but I love a little scratch on that spot behind my ears—y'know, right there. The best."

The kitty moved a little closer, warming up to Wolf with each word.

"Yeah, see?" Wolf nodded. "You know what I'm talking about."

The cat sniffed at Wolf's hand, and then she began to purr. "Yeah, who's a good kitty?" he muttered. "Who's a good kitty?" A moment later, she gently and gingerly crawled into his arms. Just as Wolf settled into the snuggle, the other Bad Guys arrived. They gaped up at their pal, who was sitting in a tree, cuddling a cat.

Wolf climbed down, the cat still nestled carefully into the crook of his arm. A warm shiver ran down his spine, all the way to his wagging tail. It felt *good*!

Webs blinked. "Wolf? You . . . saved him??"

Just then, Professor Marmalade stepped out of the bushes. He was holding his phone up. "Yes!" he cried, stopping his video recording. He'd caught the whole thing on his phone camera, and now he quickly uploaded it to the Web. "Yes, it's working!"

"You filmed that?" Wolf asked.

"Yes!" Marmalade cried happily. "And they're starting to like you. People are going to watch this video, and they'll fall in love! This might just be enough to win over the guests at the gala."

The rest of the guys cheered. "Now we're talking!" They all whooped. "All right! We did it!"

Wolf grinned. He *had* done it—he'd figured out how to crack through and start to make people think the Bad Guys really *could* be good! They all headed proudly back toward the mansion, but on the way, Marmalade pulled Wolf aside. "Wolf," he said quietly. "I must say, you've really turned a corner. You're getting it. I can see it from tip to tail." He glanced down at Wolf's still-wagging tail. "It's just a shame that you have to carry all that *baggage*."

Wolf cast a glance at the professor. "You mean the guys?"

Marmalade nodded. "You have great potential, Wolf. But at some point, you're going to have to choose between your friends . . . or the Good Life." He gave Wolf a little pat and walked away, leaving Wolf alone to consider his words.

But when they got to their bedroom a little while later, Snake called down to Wolf's bunk after all the other guys were asleep. "Hey, you still awake?" he asked Wolf. The cat Wolf had saved from the tree meowed in response, now settled into Wolf's lap. "You . . . brought the cat in?"

"Yeah." Wolf laughed uncomfortably. He didn't want to let the kitty go, now that she was safe, but he also didn't want his friends thinking he'd gone soft. "I'm just . . . saving it up for later. Why, what's up?"

"I was just getting a little worried," Snake said. "Since you've kind of become a . . ."

"Become a what?" Wolf asked, rubbing the kitten's ears.

"You know, a teacher's pet," Snake told him. "Getting all cozy with Marmalade, your tail wagging, and everything."

The cat purred, and Wolf pushed it away. "Well, yeah. Because it has to be believable."

Snake breathed a sigh of relief. He'd heard what Marmalade had said to Wolf earlier in the night, and he was worried the professor's words had gotten to his friend.

"Uh-huh," Snake muttered. "Yeah, I guess so. As long as it's all part of the plan." Snake slid down from his upper bunk to confront Wolf. "It *is* all part of the plan . . . isn't it?"

"Snake. Buddy," Wolf said, trying to reassure his friend. "Who made the plan to begin with?"

"You did," Snake said.

"So I'm the one who sticks to the plan the most, right?"

"Yeah, right," Snake agreed, reluctantly. "I guess that makes sense. But if the plan were ever to *change*, you'd tell me. Right?"

"Snake, you have my word," Wolf promised. Snake looked somewhat relieved. Wolf stuck his fist out for Snake to bump with his head. Wolf grinned. "Go bad . . ." he began.

"Or go home," Snake finished. Then he slithered back up to his bunk, hoping this would be the end of it.

But a moment later, Wolf called out into the darkness, "Hey, Snake. You ever wonder what it'd be like? The world loving us instead of being scared of us? You ever think of that?"

"Loving us?" Snake scoffed. "Yeah, right. I don't waste time thinking about stuff that's never gonna happen." He sighed. "I can't wait for things to get back to normal."

"Yeah," Wolf said. "Back to normal. Back to normal."

CHAPTER ELEVEN

The next afternoon, the Bad Guys prepared for their big night as early coverage of that evening's gala filled TV screens across the city.

Tiffany Fluffit was first on the scene of the charity event, reporting live from the red carpet, a few hours before the start of the festivities. "We are just minutes away from Marmalade's Gala for Goodness, where the legendary Love Crater Meteorite—the city's symbol of hope—will be on display for the first time ever!" she said, smiling into the camera.

Tiffany's face disappeared from the screen as a producer cut to pre-recorded footage of the meteorite being lowered onto a special pedestal onstage, in a place of prominence for the evening's festivities. "But what *everyone* is really buzzing about," Tiffany said over the footage, "is the Bad Guys . . . whose heartwarming rescue video has made them an overnight viral sensation."

The coverage switched to on-the-ground interviews with people on the street, who were reacting to the video of Wolf saving the kitten from the tree. "I've never been a cat person *or* a wolf person," one lady cooed. "But now I'm both!"

"I have a cat," a second person said into the camera. "And that video really brought us together. That could have been my cat. It could have been any of our cats!"

"I'm literally thinking about throwing my cat in a tree," said a third person being interviewed by a reporter, "just so the Bad Guys can come rescue her! If loving cats makes you a Bad Guy, then lock me up!"

Meanwhile, inside Marmalade's limo, the Bad Guys were thinking about everything *other* than saving more cats. "Okay, guys," Wolf said, drawing the other guys in close. "This is the big one." He explained the challenge that lay ahead of them, considering the extra protections that were in place for the Golden Dolphin statue after their *last* heist attempt. "The Golden Dolphin is inside a titanium case controlled by a randomly generated five-digit code—a code kept safe and secure inside a briefcase, handcuffed to the chief of police."

Piranha whistled. "She's not messing around, is she?"

Wolf shook his head. "The code is only accessible with her authorized fingerprint."

"Leave that to me," Snake assured the others.

"While Snake gets the code," Wolf went on, "Shark will secure the fake dolphin. There will be plenty of lookalikes sitting on the tables."

"I like the sound of that." Shark smiled.

"Meanwhile, the rest of us plant circuit jammers around the gala . . ." Wolf explained.

". . . allowing me to hack into the power grid," Webs said.

"At the end of the night," Wolf went on. "We toast the professor. Blah blah blah, yadda yadda yadda . . . and when I say 'Marmalade,' I hit the switch, lights go out, and we'll have exactly *four* seconds to make our move."

Snake chuckled. "The ol' switcheroo . . ." He could already imagine their moment of glory: He'd enter the code to crack into the titanium case, it would open, and they—the Bad Guys—would swap the Golden Dolphin for a dummy dolphin. They'd close the case back up, quick and easy, and the lights would be back on again. No one the wiser . . . except the Bad Guys! They'd be loooong gone before anyone realized what had happened.

"So," Wolf said, cutting into the end of Snake's daydream. "Chief hands Marmalade his *fake* dolphin, we get our pardon, everyone cheers, applause applause, exit stage right, and then—"

"SO LONG, SUCKERS!!" A pre-programmed, mocking GIF of Wolf lowering a pair of sunglasses onto his face flashes across the screens onstage, just after they'd made their hasty exit: It was a perfect farewell, from a group of perfect criminals.

Wolf nodded, proud of the plan. "By the time they realize

what happened, we'll be driving off into the sunset, badder than ever, legacy cemented."

"I gotta hand it to you," Snake said to Wolf as Webs handed out circuit jammers. "You're a real artist."

Just then, Marmalade flung open the limo door, greeting the Bad Guys from the edge of the red carpet. "Well, Good Guys, this is it!" the little guinea pig said, leaning into the limo. "Good luck out there. Remember, all eyes will be on *you* tonight, not me." He stepped aside, ushering them out into the crowd. Reporters and fans began to crowd around as they hopped out, and Marmalade announced, "They steal hearts instead of wallets now. Friends, meet THE GOOD GUYS!" There was a long, silent pause before the crowd broke into applause.

"Uh . . ." Snake said, weirded out by the applause and attention. "This is different."

"Is this a prank?" Piranha asked, a fake smile plastered on.

Shark stepped backward. "What's that sound? It's like screaming but not terrified."

Wolf spoke calmly to the gang, "Just roll with it."

Webs hopped out of the limo and whooped. "It's crime time, baby!"

The Bad Guys—aka Good Guys—were immediately swallowed up by the crowd. Fans wanted to take pictures with them, people wanted to ask for their advice, and everyone simply wanted to be near the city's newest celebrities. "Ms. Tarantula!" one partygoer called out. "Any advice for the young hackers out there?"

"Uh . . ." Webs answered tentatively. "Grow more legs?"

Dodging the crowd, Shark focused on his first task. "Fake dolphin . . ." he muttered, while scanning the party area. "Find fake dolphin . . . bingo!" He raced toward the replica dolphin statue, but before he could get to it, he was mobbed by a crowd of fans.

"Is it true sharks can smell blood a mile away?" someone shouted to him.

"What? No!" Shark said, cringing. "That's freaky."

"Mr. Piranha!" someone shouted on the other side of the room. "Can I get a selfie?"

"Mr. Wolf!" someone else hollered. "I loved your video!"

The crowd was going *nuts* for the Good Guys. Marmalade had been totally right when he'd said all eyes would be on them tonight. It was going to be challenging to execute their plan with so many people cramming around them, keeping them from doing their important work.

From a distance, the chief of police was watching the Bad Guys through a pair of binoculars. "Okay, Wolf . . . what are you up to?" She took off her sunglasses and propped them up on the locked briefcase she'd set on the table next to her.

Lucky for Snake, the chief was blissfully unaware that he

had crawled up the side of the briefcase. While her attention was focused on the other Bad Guys she was watching through her binoculars, Snake fogged up the frame of her sunglasses with his breath—revealing a thumb print! He placed the print on the scanner of the briefcase, and it clicked open. Snake smirked—his part of the plan had been done to perfection.

The police chief called into her radio, "With criminals like this, you've got to be crafty, subtle, *invisible*. And then, the moment they let their guard down—*whammo!* You spring the trap!"

Throughout her little speech, Snake had been using his tail to dig through the insides of the briefcase to try to find the code that would unlock the case. But as soon as the chief said *whammo!* she slammed her briefcase closed—trapping Snake's tail inside. He tried to yank it out, but it was full-on stuck inside the case.

Snake let out a high-pitched squeal.

The chief swiped the briefcase up and headed for the bar—with a trapped Snake dangling from the case at her side. She signaled for the bartender to bring her a drink. "Yep, always one step ahead. I think I've earned a tonic water."

Maybe, Snake thought, his tail screaming in pain, *my part of the plan isn't going* exactly *right after all* . . .

CHAPTER TWELVE

The evening's events were officially underway, and the police chief was still on high alert—but now, even better, she had a tasty drink by her side and a perfect view of the whole room. She'd set up her command post on one end of the bar, where she could see the dance floor, and could keep her briefcase tucked behind her for safekeeping.

Snake had been trying desperately to wriggle free from the case, but so far had had no luck. Then his luck got even *worse*. The chief grabbed what she assumed to be her drink, but she had *actually* grabbed Snake around the neck instead! As she lifted her hand to take a sip of her cocktail, Snake quickly opened his mouth, pretending to be a glass. Before the chief could get Snake's mouth all the way up to her own and realize her mistake, the rest of the Bad Guys spotted Snake's predicament and rushed to help.

When she noticed the Bad Guys heading her way, the chief lowered her drink. The Bad Guys waved at her, but she just scowled in return. "That's right," she warned, her voice just higher than a whisper. "Be intimidated . . ."

Wolf suddenly noticed Piranha dashing away. Shark, Tarantula, and Wolf exchanged a look—what was he up to *now*?

The chief lifted her "glass" again, preparing to take a swig from Snake's mouth. But before she could put her lips to Snake's, Piranha crooned into a microphone, "*Loooook at me!*" He'd jumped onstage and begun to sing. Clearly, he was trying to draw everyone's—but specifically the chief's—attention away from Snake's predicament. The chief lowered her drink, watching as Shark ran over to the stage, grabbed a drumstick, and started to hit a cowbell. Webs lowered herself onto the turntable, also getting into the musical mood. Piranha continued to sing, "*Tell me whaaaaat you see!*"

The police chief finally set Snake down, which allowed him to wriggle away from her hand. He then breathed on his own neck, revealing the chief's thumbprint, and scanned it on the briefcase lock. The case popped open, and he squiggled free. But before he fled, he also grabbed hold of an envelope inside the case, opened it, and read the code tucked inside: "1 2 3 4." *Really?* Snake thought, shaking his head. *Real secret code, Chief.*

He slyly slipped the letter back in the envelope, dropped it in the briefcase, and flashed the rest of the Bad Guys a thumbs-up. As soon as they saw that he'd gotten away and had the code, the three onstage hopped offstage and began to mingle around the crowd, still singing their song.

As Wolf made his way to the stage to join his friends, he felt a hand on his shoulder. Diane's voice was immediately recognizable. "Ah, Mr. Wolf," she said.

"Oh . . . Diane," Wolf said nervously. He felt weird around her, ever since their last conversation. "What a surprise!"

Diane looked at him curiously. "If I didn't know better," she said, tilting her head. "I'd think that you were avoiding me." She smiled, and Wolf turned away.

"Avoiding you?" Wolf asked. In truth, he *had* been avoiding her. But he was surprised she had noticed. He grinned, trying to brush her off as he backed away.

Then, as he began his walk to the stage again, she called after him. "I have to say . . . I'm a little disappointed."

Wolf cocked his head, somewhat worried about where she was going with this.

"I was hoping," the governor said, "you were going to ask me to dance." Wolf grinned at her, and Diane spun him onto the dance floor. They dragged other partygoers up with them, welcoming everyone onto the dance floor to party. Wolf whipped out a few of his most classic dance moves, and Diane laughed. "I see you lost the sheep's clothing."

Wolf grinned back at her. "Yeah, I figured it was time I got comfortable in my own fur."

Using the chaos on the dance floor as a diversion, the rest

of the gang began to carry out their heist. The sheer number of people moving and grooving around the party would make it nearly impossible for anyone to suspect they were doing anything wrong. One by one, each of the Bad Guys took turns placing their transmitters in the designated spots. Webs set a fob on the DJ's computer and started to hack into the main system.

Meanwhile, the crowd continued to dance. Diane and Wolf moved elegantly around the dance hall together, swooping past other guests who were all having a great time. As they made their way through the room, Wolf surprised the governor by dropping his wallet into a donation box near the front door. "I think I like the new you," she said, lifting one eyebrow.

"Well, that makes two of us," he shot back, surprising himself.

Following Wolf's lead, more and more guests began to add their own cash to the donation boxes that had been set up around the room for the evening's charity event. On-screen near the stage, the digital donation counter started growing at a frenzied pace. There were a series of benchmarks Marmalade had set up to try to gauge the success of the night's event. The count quickly passed GIANT, then STUPENDOUS, then RIDICULOUS, then RIDONKULOUS . . . it was climbing higher and higher by the second.

Tiffany Fluffit noticed the donation count jumping up and grabbed her cameraman. "Quick!" she told him. "On me . . ." As soon as the camera was running, she grinned and said, "Here at Marmalade's charity event, we're going to need to break out our umbrellas because it is raining . . . money!" She beamed into the camera. "All because of—I can't believe I'm saying this—the BAD GUYS!"

Meanwhile, across the room, Tiffany—and every other guest at the event—had no idea Webs was busy hacking away at the power grid through her laptop while Shark sauntered over to the fake dolphin statue and slipped it into his suit. Diane was as oblivious as the rest of the crowd, still too busy dancing with Wolf to notice that anything bad was happening right under her nose. "So, Wolf," she said as they foxtrotted across the room. "How does it feel to have everyone not fear you for a change?"

Her question caught Wolf off guard. He hadn't even thought about it, but now that she mentioned it . . . "It feels . . . good," Wolf said, noticing a shiver up his spine as his tail began to wag. "Real good."

Diane beamed at him. Just then, Snake winked at Wolf to signal that the heist was officially underway. Webs had finished her hack, and now it was time to set the next part of their plan into motion. Wolf pulled Diane's diamond ring out of his pocket. He was kind of torn about *everything*

now, but at least this was something he could fix. "Diane," he began. "I want to give this back. It belongs to you." He took her hands in his and dropped the ring into her open palms.

While the rest of the Bad Guys moved to their marks, Wolf maneuvered the governor to the stage, right next to the Golden Dolphin, just as the donation counter hit $1 billion. The crowd erupted in applause, confetti fell from the rafters, and Marmalade took the stage to address his guests. "The money raised tonight will be delivered tomorrow to local schools, hospitals, and other worthy causes across the city!"

The crowd went wild, and Wolf felt—not for the first time that week—a pit in his stomach. The cheering, the clapping, the adoration . . . all that goodness. It did feel good. Was their heist really the right thing to do right now? Shark nudged Wolf from behind. He was up. Strolling toward center stage, Wolf grabbed the mic and Snake slid up beside the Golden Dolphin case.

"Thanks, everybody. You're too kind," Wolf began, pulling out the switch that would cut the lights, so they could make the switcheroo from real Golden Dolphin to the fake. He locked eyes with Diane, Marmalade, and guests in the crowd—who were all cheering for him. "I just want to take a moment to recognize the one responsible for our new outlook . . ." This was where he was supposed to say "Marmalade" and hit the trigger.

But all of a sudden, Wolf knew he couldn't do it. His finger hovered over the button, but the cheers, the love, the wag—it was too much.

"Come on . . ." Shark urged in a whisper.

". . . our brilliant mentor," Wolf squeaked out.

"Do it," Snake hissed.

". . . a paragon of enlightenment," Wolf said, trying to fish for more time.

"Do it!" Webs growled.

"The one and only . . . Professor . . ." Wolf knew he couldn't stall much longer before stuff got *really* weird. "Professor . . . Professor . . ."

Piranha wondered aloud, "What is he *waiting* for?"

Wolf was now sweating like crazy. He couldn't make his friends *and* Diane and the rest of the world happy at the same time. He couldn't be a Bad Guy *and* a Good Guy. He had to choose, and now was the moment for that choice. Finally, he lifted his finger off the trigger switch and finished, "Professor Marmalade!"

As soon as he said the word, the police chief typed in the code to open the trophy case.

"Chief," Wolf asked her. "May I do the honors?"

"Uh," the chief said, looking from Wolf to the Golden Dolphin and back again. "Okay."

Wolf gently cradled the statue in his hands and then

passed it over to Professor Marmalade. The other Bad Guys were stunned. "What. Is. Happening?" Tarantula gasped.

"That's not the plan," Piranha added.

"He's gone rogue!" Shark moaned.

Though his friends were upset, the crowd was delighted. Everyone was whooping and cheering, and it was all for the Wolf and the Good Guys! "A deal's a deal," Diane said into the mic, smiling. "I don't break promises. By the power vested in me, it is a pleasure to grant the Bad Guys a *full* pardon—"

Just as she said those words, the lights flipped off. *Ker-chunk*!

Wolf looked around, confused. He'd set down his trigger switch, but the lights had most definitely flicked off for a few seconds. "That was weird," he mused.

Suddenly, someone in the audience screamed, "The meteorite! It's gone!"

"Somebody stole it!" yelled someone else.

All around the room, people gasped and began talking. When Wolf looked at the spot where the famous Love Crater Meteorite had been sitting all night, he could see that what people were saying was true: It was gone. The pedestal was empty.

Naturally, everyone turned to glare at the Bad Guys. The police chief yelled, "Wolf!" and began to stride across the room.

"What?!" Wolf barked. "We didn't do it!" He glanced at his partners-in-crime. "Did we?"

"No!" Snake said.

"Chief," Wolf argued. "You can't possibly think—"

Just then, the pre-programmed GIF of a mocking Wolf lowering his sunglasses flashed onstage and the crowd heard Wolf's pre-recorded voice blare out: "So long, suckers!"

Snake screamed, "Run!" just as the crowd—and the police chief—lunged for them.

All five of the Bad Guys made a break for it. They dodged cops and guests, zigzagging through the party like the expert escape artists they were. As he ran past a table, Wolf grabbed one of the fundraiser flyers and hastily made a mark on the charity map. Then he beelined toward Diane, handing it to her. "Here—" he said, out of breath.

"What are you doing?" Diane asked.

"I'm giving it all back," Wolf told her. Then he ran as the cops closed in on him and the guys.

Snake caught up to Wolf as they continued to dodge cops on their quest to flee the event. He said, "What happened back there?"

"I couldn't do it," Wolf replied. He'd *tried*, he'd *planned* to go through with the heist, but at the last minute, he'd frozen.

"What do you mean you *couldn't do it*?" Snake mocked.

Just then, Piranha stopped in his tracks. "No!" he shouted, turning back. "I do not run. That is not how I roll!"

"Piranha," Wolf cautioned. "Don't do anything crazy . . ."

Taking a heroic stance, Piranha pointed out, "'Crazy' is what I bring to the party, *chico*." He pulled out the team's grappling hook and fired it into the air. It wasn't until the hook went flying up into open sky that Piranha remembered they were outside. The hook had nothing to attach to, so it came hurtling back to the ground and landed with a *plunk!* right on Shark's head. He spun in a slow circle, then collapsed.

All the other Bad Guys stared at the hook, a downed Shark, then glanced at Piranha. There was an awkward pause while they all just stood there—then they each slowly held up their hands as the cops closed in around them.

CHAPTER THIRTEEN

BAD GUYS ARRESTED: LIFE NOT AT ALL LIKE A MOVIE

"Hey!" Wolf cried, struggling as he was dragged by the ear into a police transport. All his friends were in the same boat, each of them getting pulled and shoved into the back of the armored vehicle. "You're making a mistake! We didn't do it! I know we always say that, but this time it's actually true!"

The police chief stuffed her fingers in her ears. "Lalalalala! Can't hear you! Oh, now you are done forever, Wolf!!" She slammed the door on him, sealing Wolf and his friends into the back of the van.

"Talk to Marmalade!" Wolf screamed out, hoping he could be heard through the door. "We're really good now! Professor!"

Outside the van, Tiffany Fluffit was reporting on the scene. "Tonight's headline," she said somberly, "is that change is impossible, you should always judge a book by its cover, and all stereotypes have been affirmed."

"Stop!" Marmalade screeched. "For goodness sake!" He

popped out of the throngs of people who'd been blocking his way. "Let me speak to them," he said, breathless. "I'm sure there's been some misunderstanding."

Reluctantly, the chief of police swung open the door to the police transport.

Wolf breathed a sigh of relief. "Ah! Professor Marmalade!"

"You've got five minutes," the chief warned them. "No deals this time!" She slammed the door shut again, sealing Marmalade inside the police van with the Bad Guys.

"You have to help us," Wolf pleaded. "Tell 'em we didn't do it."

"There, there," Marmalade cooed. "Of *course* you didn't do it . . . how could you? After all," he said, patting Wolf on the hand. "You're such a *good boy*."

Wolf flinched. He'd heard those words before . . . but where? Staring at Marmalade, it suddenly hit him: It was at the Good Samaritan Awards, when he'd bumped into the old lady and saved her from falling. She'd called him a *good boy*, in the exact same tone of voice! That's when he remembered something else Marmalade had said, earlier that very night: *All eyes will be on you tonight. Not me.* Right then, Wolf realized something. He turned to Professor Marmalade, his eyes wide. "You . . . it was all you."

"What are you talking about, Wolf?" Webs asked.

"The old lady, the Golden Dolphin, 'good' training," Wolf

explained to the others. "It was all to get us HERE . . . so Marmalade himself could steal the meteorite and let *us* take the fall."

"Whoa. What old lady?" Snake asked. "And why would a guinea pig want a meteorite anyway?"

Marmalade began to laugh maniacally. "Hehehehehe!"

"Guys," Shark said nervously. "He's creeping me out."

Piranha, who was hanging by chains on the back wall of the van, had accidentally spun around so he couldn't see anything that was happening in the van anymore. "What is going on? Someone turn me around!"

"Well, well," Marmalade said, his face covered in an evil grin. "You finally get it."

"Wait," Shark said, slowly piecing things together. "So . . . *you* stole the meteorite?!"

"Oh, it's not *just* a meteorite," Marmalade told him.

Piranha looked excited. "I told you guys it's a BUTT!"

"IT'S NOT A BUTT!" Marmalade screamed. "It's the ultimate power source! You see, when it struck the city, scientists found that it emitted a powerful electromagnetic frequency, unlike anything else on Earth." He chuckled. "I'm going to harness its power to pull off the greatest heist the world has ever seen!"

"Wait . . ." Piranha and Snake both said.

Shark blurted out, "Whaaaaat?"

Webs turned to Snake and groaned. "You should have eaten him when you had the chance!"

"Yup," Snake said, nodding.

"But why *us*?" Wolf asked.

"Because you're the perfect patsies!" Marmalade said gleefully. "Come on: When people look up 'bad' in the dictionary, do they see a sweet, adorable guinea pig? No. They see *you*. And they always will." He struck a cute and innocent pose, immediately proving his point.

"Okay, fine," Snake agreed, finally putting all the pieces together. "But you set us up!"

Marmalade rolled his eyes. "Oh, pish-pish. Let's be honest: Evolution set you up. But Wolfie here really clinched it." He turned to Wolf, his smile growing even wider. "You fell for every one of my traps . . . starting with *saving* a helpless little old lady."

"Wolf?" Snake said, turning on his friend. "What's he talking about?"

"Whoopsie," Marmalade said, covering his tiny mouth. "Did I say too much? Anyhoo, looks like, yet again, the big bad wolf got outsmarted by a little piggie . . ."

"You little pouchy-cheeked rat!" Wolf howled with anger. "I'll kill you! Do you hear me? You're DEAD. You're—"

Just as Wolf lunged toward Marmalade, his mouth open and fangs bared, Marmalade popped open the back door of the police van. Screaming for the benefit of the gathered crowd, Marmalade cried, "Help, oh, help! The Big Bad Wolf! Wolf is attacking me!"

The police chief rushed forward. "Oh no. You are done *forever*, Wolf!"

The crowd drew back in horror. As the chief slammed the door on Wolf's startled face, Wolf caught one final glimpse of Diane, who looked utterly disappointed. In him. She had expected more, and now she was let down. Letting someone down did not feel good.

As soon as the police van pulled away from the event, Tiffany Fluffit raced to get the first interview with Professor Marmalade. "Professor! Professor! Any thoughts on how the Bad Guys managed to steal the meteorite in plain sight?"

Marmalade shook his head. "Well, off the top of my head—perhaps they accessed the site previously and set up an intricate system of tunnels and trapdoors that could be remotely triggered to suck the meteorite down into a holding area . . ." He shrugged. "But how should I know? They're the deranged masterminds, not me!"

Diane watched the interview with interest. Something wasn't adding up. As she walked away, she pulled out the flyer Wolf had handed her during the chase. She scanned the map and noticed that Wolf had marked a specific area on the map with a big X.

It seemed Diane was holding a treasure map . . . and she intended to follow it and get to the bottom of this.

A short while later, in the empty river basin outside Wolf's secret lair, the governor entered a tunnel that led to a hidden apartment. She'd followed the map to the X, and this is where it had led her. When the elevator doors opened, Diane stepped out and into Wolf's secret lair. Inside, she found every single thing the Bad Guys had stolen over the years. There were statues, paintings, tapestries, safes, gold bars, jewels.

Diane let out a low whistle. "Whoa . . ." This was incredible. Wolf had given her this map, and it led her straight here. She couldn't believe it . . . was it possible? Had she actually gotten through to him? Was Wolf actually . . . trying to be *good*?

CHAPTER FOURTEEN

The Bad Guys were being loaded into a military-grade police boat. This boat would deliver them to the highest-security prison for thousands of miles—far offshore, on a prison island.

Meanwhile, the Bad Guys were *wishing* they were back home, surrounded by all their treasures, right about now. But thanks to a double-crossing guinea pig, they were on their way to the most high-security prison on Earth instead of riding off into the sunset scot-free with the Golden Dolphin.

"I can't believe we got double-crossed by a tiny, adorable rodent." Shark moaned.

"Oh, we got double-crossed by a rodent, all right," Snake grumbled. Then he glanced in Wolf's direction. "But not by a tiny one."

The other Bad Guys gasped when they realized what Snake was saying: that Wolf had set them up, and all this was his fault. Snake was blaming Wolf for getting them all caught!

"This was supposed to be us conning Marmalade," Snake

said. "It turns out it was Wolf conning us! Does that sound familiar to you, Wolf?"

"What?" Wolf barked. "Why would you think that?"

Snake tipped his head. "Oh, I don't know . . . maybe because you just *sabotaged* the biggest heist of our lives! I think you owe us an explanation, buddy."

Guards began unloading them into the processing room. "Okay, okay," Wolf said as they all got fingerprinted. "This is what happened: Back at the museum, I tried to steal an old lady's purse. Classic snatch and grab."

"Tried to?" Tarantula said, pressing her fifth set of fingers to the pad before moving on to hands six, seven, and eight. "Since when do you *try* to steal something and not just *steal* it?"

"I was trying to steal the purse when the old lady fell," Wolf explained as they watched the cops send a few guys through a pat down to check for weapons. "And so I just helped her out a little bit."

"Sorry?" Snake called out from where he was posing for a mug shot. "What was that?"

"I kind of . . . helped her," Wolf said. He took Snake's place and now he was grinning for the police booking camera.

Piranha scooted through a metal detector. "But *then* you stole the purse?" he asked nervously.

Wolf took a deep breath as he stepped forward to take his

turn getting searched. "No, I saved the old lady, and she hugged me, and my tail wagged. I didn't know what it was, but it felt . . . uh . . . y'know . . . *good*!"

All four of the other Bad Guys stopped what they were doing and turned to stare at their fearless leader. "Ah," Piranha said, finally breaking the silence. "But *then* you stole the purse?"

The others all stared daggers at him, wondering how it was possible that Piranha *still* didn't get it. "NO!" they all screamed.

Snake glared at Wolf. "I heard what the pig said to you last night, about cutting us loose."

"Like, *us* us?" Webs blurted.

"Pig said what?" Piranha asked.

"He didn't!" Shark gasped. "That is *not* okay."

"But I never thought you'd actually do it," Snake said, accusingly.

"I would never—" Wolf argued. "I was just trying to find us a better life!"

Snake frowned. "Our life was perfect. Until you decided to ruin it!"

"I didn't!" Wolf promised as they were led to a holding cell in the prison. "C'mon, you guys felt it at the gala—the clapping, the cheering—we were more than just scary villains. They loved us!"

Shark, Piranha, and Webs shared a look. Wolf could tell that they'd felt it, too. He wasn't the only one who had liked the attention.

"Oh yeah?" Snake said. "If they 'loved us' so much, then how come we're in prison for a crime we didn't commit?" Wolf looked down. Snake had him there. "You know what? I'll give Marmalade this. At least he sees the world for what it is—a place where some people are scary . . . and some people are *scared*."

"Well, I'm tired of being scary!" Wolf said. "I'm tired of being an outcast. Maybe I don't want to be—"

"What?" Snake said, cutting him off. "A Bad Guy?"

The others spun around to stare at Wolf. Surely that's not what he was saying . . . or was it?

"Say it, Wolf," Snake demanded. When Wolf said nothing, Snake shook his head. "I thought so . . . and us, your lifelong friends—we're just holding you back."

Wolf heaved a sigh. "Well, maybe you are!" The instant he said it, Wolf knew he'd gone too far. Snake leaped at Wolf, who snarled and flashed his fangs and claws at his bestie.

"Take it back!" Snake ordered. "Take it back! Apologize!"

A prison guard stepped toward them, holding up a weapon as he growled, "Hey hey hey! Prison is no place for fighting!"

Suddenly, another guard fell from the ceiling. With a moan, he pointed upward. "Tell that to him."

"Huh?" Wolf said, looking up.

Just then, a mysterious, masked, ninja-like figure leaped out of the shadows on an upper ledge and jumped into the Bad Guys' cell. As soon as the rest of the guards spotted the intruder, they charged. But the stranger had no trouble fighting the guards off with some incredible martial arts skills.

As soon as the guards had been knocked aside, all rendered unconscious, the mysterious stranger then turned to the Bad Guys and began slicing open their metal chains to set them free. "Wait, wait, wait," Wolf said. "Hold on, wait a second—"

As soon as they'd all been cut loose, the stranger unmasked herself. It was Governor Diane Foxington!

"But . . ." Piranha said, mind totally blown by what had just happened. "How do you know how to do all that . . . kick-kick, punch-punch stuff?"

"Wait a sec . . ." Wolf said, stepping toward her. He'd seen those moves before. But if Diane could fight like that, that meant: "You're the . . . the . . . Crimson Paw. Maestro of mischief. Acrobatic Swiss Army knife. Stole the Zumpango Diamond *twice*—once for profit, second time just for fun? Never identified, never caught."

Diane grinned, putting her hands on her hips. "Guess I'm still the best bad guy the world has ever seen." Just then, she noticed a tiny rip in her uniform. She shrugged. "At least I used to be."

Before they could ask her questions about her secret double identity, a sea of armed guards came racing down the corridor. It was obviously time for them to hit the road—or they'd be stuck in prison forever. All of them. As the Bad Guys screamed in terror, Diane let out a crazed battle cry and whipped out a few insane martial arts moves, hurtling *toward* the guards so the Bad Guys could run away.

A few minutes later, they were all racing away from the prison on a motorboat, guards left useless in their wake. Diane brushed the debris off her Crimson Paw suit as they sped away. "Nope, I'm still the best. It's just like riding a stolen bicycle."

"But . . ." Wolf said, shocked by this insane secret they'd just learned about Diane . . . aka the Crimson Paw. "Why did you save us, anyway?"

Diane told them, "After the gala, I knew something wasn't right. So, I did some investigating, and that meteor—"

"We know," Wolf said, cutting her off. "It's some kind of cosmic-mega-super-antenna-thingy."

"Right!" Diane nodded. "If conducted through an array of ionized crystals, it will generate a massive psychokinetic field the size of a city!" She glanced at Wolf, only then realizing she'd stolen his thunder. "Oh my gosh, were you going to say that?"

"Actually, I was gonna be a little more technical." Wolf coughed to hide his lie. "But you got the gist of it."

When their escape boat pulled up to shore, Diane hopped out and told the Bad Guys what they already knew all-too-well. "Marmalade needs to be stopped. But I can't do it alone. You know his compound better than—"

Wolf grabbed Diane's paw. "You can count on us." He turned to his friends. "Right, guys?"

"Uh . . ." Snake said. "What do you mean *us*? There is no *us*. We're through, Wolf. Done. *Finito!*"

"Because of that little tiff back there?" Wolf asked. "C'mon, that's what we do. You serve, I volley. That's our little dance."

"Not this time." Snake spat. Then he skulked off, waiting for the others to follow.

Wolf glanced at Shark, Piranha, and Webs. None of them moved. How were they supposed to pick sides? They were a team, a unit, partners. They were in this *together*. "Piranha?" Wolf asked.

Piranha turned his back on Wolf and wandered over to join Snake.

"Webs?"

"Sorry, Wolfie," Tarantula said, heading over to Snake's side.

". . . Shark?"

Shark glanced at Wolf for a while before clenching his jaw and turning away. Wolf could hear him sobbing quietly as he moved to stand by Snake. They'd all picked sides, and they hadn't picked Wolf.

"Hey," Wolf tried one last time. "Guys! Guys . . . ?"

Snake spun around to give Wolf one last piece of his mind. "You want to know why I hate birthdays? Do you? When you grow up a snake, nobody shows up to your party. Birthdays are a constant reminder that, out there, I'm just a scary, good-for-nothing monster." He glared at Wolf. "But nothing compares to having the one guy I thought I could trust stab me in the back." He gestured for the rest of the Bad Guys to follow him. "C'mon, guys."

Wolf stood beside Diane, watching as his best friends in the whole world walked away—leaving him all alone with no idea what he was going to do next.

CHAPTER FIFTEEN

Back at Marmalade's evil compound, very bad things were afoot. While Marmalade watched on, his servant Cuddles used a small crane to lower the meteorite into a large device that looked like a battery compartment. As soon as it was in place, Marmalade powered up the device, and the meteorite began to emit a toxic pink glow.

Nothing says *evil* like a toxic pink glow.

Marmalade chuckled. "Now, this is what a true bad guy looks like," he said, strapping on a strange helmet. He flipped a switch on the helmet, and the helmet lit up—using the power of the meteorite. "What do you say we have some fun?" he said, cackling. "Hehehehehehe!"

In front of Marmalade, there was a giant cage holding an innocent guinea pig. Marmalade focused intently, and in a matter of seconds his brain waves began to emit from the helmet. The guinea pig's eyes began to turn red. Marmalade raised his arms, and the guinea pig stood up. Marmalade beamed. His mind-control helmet was working!

He cranked up the power, and a few minutes later, he was

controlling hundreds of guinea pigs he'd released across the city, using the power of the meteorite. Under their evil leader's mind-control power, they formed into groups, which merged into bigger groups, until there were full armies marching through the city. On Marmalade's command, they began to dive into manholes, crawl through sewer lines, and infiltrate the whole of Los Angeles.

Meanwhile, across town, Snake, Webs, Shark, and Piranha returned to their lair, only to find that the place had been completely emptied in their absence. Diane had cleared the place out, removing every single stolen item they'd worked so hard to acquire over the past few years. "All our stuff!" Piranha wailed.

"Wha—" Snake said, not getting it at first. "Where is everything? It's ALL gone!"

Shark raced to open a closet door on the far side of the room, horrified to find it empty. "My disguise closet!"

"Where's my things?" Tarantula said, her breath coming quicker and quicker with each look around the room.

"Wolf gave away all our loot?!" Snake asked. He couldn't believe their buddy would turn on them like this. He'd gone *all out* to ruin them. "Years of work! We stole that stuff, fair and square!"

Piranha suddenly lost it and went totally nuts. "Now I understand what it feels like to have things stolen *from* you! I. Don't. Like. It!"

Webs wandered over to her pal, trying to comfort him. At first, Piranha was surprised by the unexpected gesture—but after a second, he realized he kind of liked the feeling of someone taking care of him.

Frustrated and exhausted, Snake wandered over to the fridge. The only thing still left in their secret lair were the photo memories pinned to the outside of the fridge with magnets. He angrily pulled open the fridge to see if there was anything left inside—and found one last, lonely push pop. He eyed it, deciding that the only thing that might cool the sting of his friend's betrayal was a nice, cold push pop.

But before he could pop it in his mouth, Shark wailed from across the room. "We have no food! No money we can use to buy food! No food we can sell for money!"

Without a second thought, Snake handed Shark the final push pop to try to console him. "Alright, okay," Snake said hastily. "Here, here. Take this. Now stop crying, buddy."

Shark grabbed the pop and began to slurp it happily, until he suddenly realized what had just happened. Both Shark and Tarantula stared at Snake, totally dumbfounded.

"Um . . ." Webs said slowly. "Snake? What did you just do?"

"What?" Snake snapped. "My friend was sad, so I cheered him up."

"You—" Shark said, still sobbing a few leftover tears, "you did a good thing. For me?"

Snake froze. "Don't be ridiculous," he spat out. "I just put your needs before my own."

Webs nodded. "Yeah, you're being good."

"I'm not!" Snake insisted. "I was simply making a sacrifice so Shark could be happy."

Tarantula held up one hand. "That *is* the actual definition of being good."

"Snake!" Shark cheered. "You! The worst one of us. The most selfish—"

"Spiteful!" Tarantula added.

"Terrible!" Shark went on.

"Sneaky!" said Piranha.

"Dishonest!" Tarantula continued.

Shark put in, "Insensitive!"

"Manipulative!" Tarantula noted.

"Snakelike!" Piranha yelped.

"Stanky!" said Shark.

Snake glared at them all. "And your point is?"

"Wolf's right," Tarantula said. "Maybe we *could* be more than just scary villains?" Just then, she noticed Shark's fin, Piranha's mohawk, and her own tummy wiggling from side to side. "Oh, wow. Is this wagging? We're . . . we're WAGGING!"

Snake noticed his own tail had also started wagging.

"I'm feeling," Piranha said joyfully, "tingly all over! I got a tingle!"

Snake glanced at his own tail. "No! NO! Stop it! We will *always* be BAD GUYS!" He slammed the fridge door shut, and all the Bad Guys' family photos fell to the floor. Snake immediately turned on his tail and stormed out.

CHAPTER SIXTEEN

"Hey," Diane said softly to Wolf as they pulled into the driveway of her house. She'd noticed Wolf had been lost deep in thought for nearly the whole drive. "You okay?"

"No," Wolf grumped. "I'm not okay! I am *very* un-okay. I just left the only friends I've ever had. What am I doing?"

Diane sighed. "I know this can't be easy. To leave everything behind."

"Do you?" Wolf snapped back.

"I was the best thief in the world," she reminded him. "Fast, fearless, inventive. I just had one thing left to steal . . ."

"The Golden Dolphin . . ." Wolf nodded. "So you went after it—"

"I didn't just go after it. I *had it*. And a clear escape route." Diane thought back to that night, how she'd had everything she thought she'd ever wanted in the palm of her hand—but then the guilt set in. The worry. The regret. "All I saw in the end was the tricky fox they always told me I was. It changed everything. So I dropped the Dolphin and left."

Wolf was shocked. This was not the legendary story he thought he knew.

"So now," she went on, "instead of hurting people, I'm helping them. I'm still me, I'm just me on the right side." She looked at Wolf seriously. "You're doing the right thing. And someday, your friends . . . if they're real friends, I think they'll understand." She reached for her car door handle. "Now, come on. Let's get inside. You look like you just busted out of a prison."

BOOM!

Before they could open their doors, several rabid-looking guinea pigs raced across the hood of Diane's car. "Were those . . . guinea pigs?" She gasped, watching in shock as they raced past and kept going.

She and Wolf exchanged a look, then together they both shouted: "Marmalade!"

"Let's bounce," said Wolf.

Diane led Wolf inside her house so they could prepare their counterattack against Marmalade and what seemed to be a crazy army of guinea pigs. "So *this* is the hideout of the great Crimson Paw, eh?" Wolf looked around, a little surprised at how . . . boring the place was.

Diane ignored him, punching numbers into her microwave.

"Snack break," Wolf noted. "Okay. Oddly timed, but you do you."

Diane gave him a sly look. Suddenly, a robotic voice chirped out of the microwave, "Identity verified. Welcome, Diane."

In the next instant, the fridge slid to the side, revealing a secret elevator that had been hidden behind the wall. They rode down, and at the bottom floor, the doors slid open to reveal an epic tactical chamber. "Whoa . . ." Wolf mused, taking it all in. Diane had more than a few secrets she was hiding! "Holy moly."

Smiling, Diane said, "I know, right? Ah, it's good to be home." She pushed a switch, and a whole bunch of amazing gadgets were lowered from the ceiling.

"Laser-sighted zipline!" Wolf exclaimed as he pawed through all the stuff. "Micro adhesive climbing mesh! The XM2400 Radar Jammer? No way!"

"I actually prefer the earlier model," Diane said, shrugging.

"Agree to disagree," Wolf replied. He reached down and grabbed a tube of lipstick. He began to playfully twirl it around in his hand, but Diane stopped him.

"That's a flamethrower," she warned. "Also, not your color."

Wolf nervously set it back down alongside all the other gadgets.

Diane perched in front of a high-tech computer console and began to type. "Marmalade . . ." she muttered to herself. "What are you up to, you fuzzy little weirdo? We need eyes on the city. Let's see if we can't hack into the government surveillance satellite."

"But you're the governor," Wolf pointed out. "Couldn't you just *ask*?"

"Yeah," Diane said, shrugging. "But the paperwork." She clicked a few buttons, activating her supercomputer. On-screen, a picture of a satellite in space flashed to life. While Wolf watched, the satellite changed directions and pointed where Diane was directing it to go—right over the city of Los Angeles. "I am definitely picking up suspicious activity here," she said. "Switching to thermal scan."

While Diane scanned the city via satellite, trying to figure out where to zoom in, Wolf picked up a Good Samaritan newsletter. Inside, there was a map of all the charities that were set to receive funds after Marmalade's charity fundraiser event.

Diane drew Wolf's attention to her computer screen. "Those are guinea pig heat signatures," she told him, pointing. She hit a button, and moments later, even more red dots appeared on-screen. She zoomed out to see more of the city, and there were even *more* red dots. "Marmalade seems to be controlling them," she said. "But to do what? There are no obvious targets."

Wolf nodded. "That's because they're *moving* targets," he told her. He set the newsletter map over the top of the map of the city on Diane's monitor. The red dots were all heading toward the schools that were waiting to get their delivery of charity money! "There's more than a billion dollars inside trucks, on their way to charities all over the city," he said aloud. Marmalade was using his army of guinea pigs to try to stop those trucks and steal the money!

"We need to cut off Marmalade's communication with his guinea pig army," Diane said.

Wolf grinned. "Hey, if there's no signal . . ."

Diane smiled back. ". . . there's no heist. Put on your big girl pants, Wolf. We're gearing up."

They both hastily grabbed the tools and gadgets they would need to stop Marmalade's evil plot. But when Wolf saw Diane reaching for a grappling hook, Wolf winced. He and his team hadn't had much luck with those lately . . . "I wouldn't take that," he cautioned. "Those things will rip your pants right off."

Diane laughed. "Try wearing clean underwear. Just in case."

As soon as they were set to go, Diane opened a set of garage doors. Wolf peeked inside and spotted the Bad Guys mobile hanging out, right in the middle of Diane's parking pad. "You *stole* my car?" He nodded appreciatively, then hopped in and revved the engine. "*Respect*."

As he settled into the driver's seat, Wolf thought to himself: *It felt so good to be back, right where he belonged.*

CHAPTER SEVENTEEN

Back in Marmalade's lair, the professor's plan was going exactly as it should. While armored cash trucks shot across the city to Marmalade's very own charity destinations, his army of mind-controlled guinea pigs were in hot pursuit. "Faster, faster, my little pigs!" Marmalade cooed from inside his mind-control helmet.

He laughed as he watched his little army on-screen. As they overtook the trucks, the cash-mobiles were each turned around and rerouted to their *new* destination, Marmalade's compound! Soon, all of that money would be his, and his alone!

But little did he know, Wolf and Diane were heading there now—and they had a plan of their own to stop him. As Wolf and Diane sped to Marmalade's compound, Diane double-checked that she and Wolf were on the same page with their plan. "Okay, once we steal the meteorite, we take it straight to the police—"

"And all will be forgiven," Wolf added.

Diane shot him a look. "I don't know about 'all.' But it's a start."

As soon as they arrived at the compound, Diane and Wolf got to work trying to sneak into the meteorite room through an opening in the ceiling. Just as they made it in and were about to grab the meteorite, Wolf noticed the Golden Dolphin—sitting on a pedestal nearby. "That's strange," Wolf mused. "Why would Marmalade just leave the Golden Dolphin here, unprotected?"

"Maybe it's a trap . . ." Diane suggested.

"Or *maybe* . . ." Wolf said, then reached out and grabbed the Golden Dolphin. But when he wrapped his hands around it, an alarm went off. "Yeah," Wolf muttered. "It was a trap." He and Diane were jolted with a blast of electric current, and everything went black.

A few minutes later, Wolf and his partner hung upside down by their feet, while Marmalade paced back and forth in front of them. He'd donned a gold-spandex jumpsuit, along with his mind-control helmet, and looked very much the part of evil villain. "Well, well . . ." he said, drumming his tiny fingers together. "If it isn't my prized pupil. And you've brought along the governor! Or should I say, *the Crimson Paw*." He flipped Diane's diamond ring up into the air, then caught it in his paw. "I have to commend you: what an ingenious way to disguise the Zumpango Diamond. Hiding it in plain sight." He flicked the diamond out of Diane's ring, and it sparkled just like the legendary diamond did—before it was stolen.

"No way!" Wolf gasped, impressed but also a little embarrassed he hadn't recognized the diamond himself.

"I'm sentimental like that." Diane shrugged.

"You always did have panache," Marmalade told her. "And yet: You still fell right into my trap."

"But how did you even know we'd be here?" Wolf asked.

"Oh, I got a little tip . . ." Marmalade said with a smile. "From a friend."

Just then, a shadow slithered up behind the professor and approached the two prisoners. Snake smirked at Wolf. "Hey, buddy," he said coolly. "How's it hanging?"

Wolf couldn't believe his best friend would double-cross him like this. To break up the Bad Guys and partner with the enemy? "Snake . . . but why?"

"Because I'm a *bad guy*, remember?" Snake said.

"Oh yeah?" Wolf said. "How's it feel working for your favorite food?"

"You're just jealous to be missing out on the heist of the century." Snake spat. "It's got everything: betrayal, a meteor, mind control . . ." He looked over at Marmalade and gestured to the mind-control helmet. "Can I try it on?"

Marmalade nodded, pulling it off. "Of course . . . *partner*!"

Snake set the helmet on his own head. "Nice," Snake said, concentrating. "All the crime, with none of the exercise."

"But why do it at all, Professor?" Diane asked Marmalade. "You've got everything!"

"Yeah," Wolf added. "And what about the 'flower of goodness'? Was it all just a lie?"

Marmalade shrugged. "Pretty much, yeah. You see, I never cared about what's 'good.' Only what's good for *me*. Like, say, a billion dollars!" He shivered, thinking about all the money heading toward him, right that very minute. "Ooh! I just got a tingle!" He giggled, then he and Snake turned to leave their prisoners so they could finish carrying out their evil scheme. "See ya, Wolfie!"

"Go bad or go home." Snake fist-bumped Marmalade. Then Marmalade gestured to his servant. "Cuddles, finish them!"

As soon as the door closed behind Snake and Marmalade, Cuddles pulled a lever and the ground under Wolf and Diane opened up—revealing a pit full of razor-sharp blades. Cuddles pressed a button, and the blades started spinning at the same time Wolf and Diane began to slowly drop down toward the grinding machine.

Diane glanced over at a pair of vents, which were now emitting a deadly looking green gas into the room. "Poison gas!" she warned Wolf. "Like the spinning blades weren't enough. Don't breathe it in!"

Cuddles panicked at the sight of the gas and was immediately knocked out by the fumes.

"I breathed it in!" Wolf wailed, beginning to panic himself. But then he paused as he got a deeper whiff of the air. "Hey . . . that's not poison gas!"

"Surprise!" Piranha shrieked as he, Shark, and Webs burst out of one of the vents on the wall.

"What?!" Wolf said, both shocked and thrilled to see his buddies. "No way! I've never been happier to smell you guys!"

"You were right, Wolfie," Webs said.

"We felt the 'wag,' man!" said Shark.

"And the tingle!" Piranha added.

"It's good, right?" Wolf said, grinning. The guys all started talking about how much they loved the feeling of their bodies wagging, how they wanted that *good* feeling all the time.

"Uh . . ." Diane broke into their warm fuzzy moment as she and Wolf drew close enough to the blades that they felt the fur on the tops of their heads being clipped. "Spinning blades!"

"Oh yeah," Shark said, all business. "Right!"

At the last possible second, Webs hit the button to stop the blades from spinning. Moments later, Diane and Wolf fell to solid ground, and Wolf rushed over to hug his friends. "Am I happy to see you guys!" With a grin, he added, "Now, let's blow this little piggie's heist down!"

CHAPTER EIGHTEEN

Wolf, Diane, and their friends slipped into the Meteorite Chamber and grabbed the Love Meteorite transmitter, just in time to overhear Marmalade outside the door saying, "And this is just the beginning! With this meteorite, we will be able to commit crimes people have only dreamed about!"

"Not bad for a butt rock," Wolf heard Snake say.

Wolf chuckled. He knew Marmalade must be fuming to hear Snake call it that. "Once again," he growled, in his weenie guinea pig voice. "It's NOT A—" Marmalade opened the door to the Meteorite Chamber, just as the Bad Guys grabbed hold of his precious rock. He pointed at them and screamed, "That's MY rock!"

"Don't mind us," Wolf said with a wave. "Just robbing this place."

The Bad Guys ran. As soon as they strapped the meteorite to the back of the car, Wolf yelled, "Tarantula, hit it!" Webs hit play on her MP3 player and the car roared forward. Wolf slowed, just as they passed the cat's tree. He leaned out the window and called, "Here, kitty, kitty!"

The cat jumped into the Bad Guy mobile, and Wolf hit the gas again. They raced toward the heart of the city, with the meteorite snuggled safely in the trunk of the car. They all whooped and hollered, proud that they had actually done it. They'd succeeded in their heist. They had *stolen* the Love Meteorite and stopped Marmalade's evil scheme! "Now to get this thing to the chief and clear your names!" Diane said.

Suddenly, Piranha glanced back over his shoulder. "Hey, *chico*," he said. "Are you sure we stopped the heist?"

Diane nodded. "Marmalade can't control the guinea pigs if he doesn't have the meteorite."

"So . . ." Piranha said, pointing to several armored vans driving full speed toward Marmalade's compound. "Who's driving those trucks?"

Wolf and Diane spun around. The meteorite was still glowing in the trunk! "Wait," Diane said, wheels spinning inside her brain. "The meteorite—"

"It's still transmitting!" Wolf hollered.

"Uh-oh," Shark moaned.

"The charity money," Wolf said, gripping the steering wheel tightly. "We've got to stop those trucks!" He turned to look at Tarantula. "Webs, is there some way to override the trucks' navigation system?"

"Sure," Webs said. "But we'd need some kind of magnetized-cross-circuit-interceptor."

Diane slyly whipped a dozen high-tech metal discs out of her suit. "You mean . . . like this?"

"Ooh!" Shark shook his head in wonder. "She just keeps getting cooler!"

Wolf guided the Bad Guy mobile into an extreme U-turn, and they chased after the money-filled trucks. It was like the good ol' days of Bad Guy cop chases, but this time, *they* were the good guys! But as Wolf continued to track the trucks, more and more trucks joined in line beside them. Soon, the Bad Guys were boxed in, part of a parade of guinea pig money trucks all heading back to Marmalade's compound. Then, all of a sudden, the trucks broke into two waves and set off in opposite directions.

"Oh no," Diane mused. "Guys, we gotta split up. Hey, Webs, you feel like a girls' trip?"

"Um . . . YES!" Webs cheered. "Later boys!"

Diane grabbed her briefcase out of the car, and Tarantula hopped up on her back. They jumped out of the Bad Guy mobile. Wolf briefly wondered what the *next* part of Diane's plan was and how she was going to get there, but then Diane opened her briefcase and a motorcycle popped out!

"I wanna go on the girls' trip," Piranha whined.

Diane and Webs split off from the others, taking an off-ramp and chasing after one set of trucks. As they passed each of the armored trucks, Webs planted a device on each one.

Meanwhile, Wolf and the other Bad Guys swerved onto another off-ramp, chasing after the rest of the fleet of trucks.

"Hey, Wolf," Piranha asked, bouncing with energy in the backseat. "Can I go crazy? Please say yes!"

"You're insured, right?" Shark asked Wolf.

"Yeah, why?" Wolf asked.

As soon as he got his *yes*, Shark ripped off the roof of the car.

Shark lifted Piranha into the air and launched him forward. "It's ceviche, baby!" Piranha whooped. The feisty fish zipped through the air, parkouring off trucks and zipping from tire to tire, planting devices on each truck he hit. Shark hung out the window, using his weight to tilt the whole car sideways on two wheels so he could reach under the trucks to plant more devices.

On Tarantula's laptop screen, the map suddenly began to populate with trucks and their trackers all across the city. "Yes!" she cheered, then got to work hacking as the final discs were put in place on the remaining trucks. Moments later, the gadgets under the trucks all began to change color. The screens inside the trucks began to flash with a message: HACKED.

The trucks' self-drive mode kicked in, and the steering wheels began to turn on their own. The guinea pigs had lost control of the trucks . . . and now they were all turning to go back in the opposite direction.

Soon the trucks were pulling up at charity locations all across the city—delivering the money to where it was *supposed* to go in the first place! The Bad Guys' plan had worked.

"Woo-hoo!" Wolf whooped. He couldn't believe they'd done it. Even though the meteorite was still transmitting, they'd hacked the trucks and thwarted Marmalade's plan to steal all the cash.

"Yeah!" Shark and Piranha said, fist-bumping each other.

Diane watched Webs work, impressed at her insane hacking skills. "Where'd you learn to do that?" she asked.

"I'm kind of a natural," Webs said. Then she whispered, "But mostly YouTube."

Diane steered her motorcycle along beside the Bad Guys' car. Webs hopped off the bike and joined the other Bad Guys in the car. "Nice work," Wolf told her.

Diane ripped off her mission suit. She was wearing her governor power suit underneath, ready to move on to the next phase of their plan. Time to turn the meteorite over to the cops. "Meet me at the police station in ten minutes," Diane said, vrooming her motorcycle. "And don't be late."

As Diane drove off, Wolf smiled at his crew. "What do you say we deliver this butt rock to the chief??" he asked, grinning.

The Bad Guys all cheered and sang while they drove full speed toward the city, with the Love Crater Meteorite tucked into the back. It was time to end this thing!

CHAPTER NINETEEN

Diane zipped to the police station as quickly as she could. Before she got too close, she flipped her motorcycle into the air and transformed it back into a briefcase. It would be waiting for her there the next time she needed it. "Chief!" she called out, striding toward the front entrance. "Thank you for getting here so quickly."

Suddenly, Tiffany Fluffit popped up, her camera crew trailing after her. "Look!" she called out. She pointed down the street, just as the Bad Guys' car careened around the corner toward the station.

"Well, butter . . . my . . . crumpets," the chief said in disbelief.

"Can it be?" Tiffany said into her microphone. "The Bad Guys are *returning* the meteorite! Perhaps this is the feel-good story we all need!"

Inside the car, the Bad Guys could already feel the excitement. "Woo-hoo!" They all cried out.

"Do you think they'll throw us a party?" Webs asked.

"Yeah," Piranha cried. "With fireworks, pinatas, and cake!"

Their smiles all dropped as soon as Piranha said *cake*. It was hard to believe they had *just* been celebrating Snake's birthday, and now they were doing all this without him. Everyone turned to look down at Snake's empty spot in the car. His birthday party hat was still crumpled up on the seat.

Wolf glanced at the other guys. This was it. The moment they had to decide. Return the meteorite because it was the *good* thing to do, or . . . sacrifice everything to try to get their pal Snake back? Wolf glanced at Diane, who was smiling at them expectantly. He looked away. Suddenly, Wolf turned to the others and said: "We can't do this without him. What do you say we take a detour first?"

Shark grinned. "He might be a Mr. Grumpypants . . ."

"But he's *our* Mr. Grumpypants," Webs finished.

Wolf floored it, leaving the police station in his dust. It was time to get their friend back.

CHAPTER TWENTY

Inside Marmalade's helicopter, the professor was now screaming at Snake. "They stole my stolen money!" he wailed. "Why did I bring you on as a partner if you can't even anticipate their next move?!"

"Oh," Snake hissed, "so all this is my fault?"

"You're probably just jealous because my heist was better than your heist!" Marmalade snapped at Snake.

"You mean, the heist where you lost the money *and* the meteorite?" Snake lifted an eyebrow.

"I'm starting to see why your friends dumped you," Marmalade snarled.

"I don't have any friends!" Snake shouted.

Just then, he heard a voice calling his name from somewhere nearby. "Snake! Snake!" Snake swiveled his head around, trying to figure out where the voice was coming from. Then, down below the helicopter, he spotted Wolf—hanging out of the Bad Guy mobile on the freeway below them—calling up to him.

Snake's eyes widened. "Wolf?"

Marmalade looked down from the chopper and noticed the meteorite, still strapped into the back of the Bad Guy mobile. "My meteorite!" he whooped.

Wolf shouted up, "Snake! Snake, come back!"

"We need you, baby!" Shark added.

Before Snake could reply, Marmalade laughed. "Oh, there you go again. Making it personal! Now, give me back my meteorite!"

"Oh yeah?" Piranha growled. "What'cha gonna do, Whiskers?"

Marmalade angrily snatched the mind-control helmet off Snake's head. "This!" Marmalade concentrated. Using the power of the meteorite, Marmalade made the ground rumble. Suddenly, a wave of guinea pigs—all obviously under control of the meteorite—burrowed out of the earth all around the Bad Guys' car. They poured onto the highway, flooding the roadways.

"We've got adorable company!" Shark said. Marmalade snapped his fingers, and the horde suddenly transformed into giant tentacles. The tentacles slammed down on the freeway as the Bad Guy mobile swerved to try to avoid being crushed. It was like they were in a giant, life-size version of a whack-a-mole game.

"Maybe I shouldn't have called him 'Whiskers,'" Piranha said.

Webs mused, "I gotta say, when I woke up this morning, this is not where I saw my day going."

Wolf continued to steer the car clear of each tentacle slap. Soon, a tower of guinea pigs approached, also trying to crash down on them—but Wolf managed to steer the car to the side.

Snake watched as Marmalade continued his attack on the Bad Guys. "Whoa," Snake said. "Let's dial this down a notch! Besides, you'll never get him. He's too good a driver."

"Hmm," Marmalade grunted. "Now that I think of it, maybe it would be better to exploit his greatest weakness."

"Exactly!" Snake agreed. "Wait, what do you mean?" Snake asked. Suddenly, Marmalade reached out and shoved Snake—hard—in the chest. He tumbled out of the helicopter.

"Nooo!" Snake cried, bouncing through the air.

"Snake!" Wolf yelled.

As he whipped and spun through the air, Snake managed to sink his fangs into the floor of the helicopter, saving himself from plummeting to certain death.

Wolf leaped into action. His friend was in danger, and he knew what he had to do. "Whoa, whoa, whoa, hold it!" he cried out. "Okay, you win. You can have the space rock."

"Good boy, Wolf," Marmalade said, sickeningly sweet. He shifted the helicopter's grappling arm so it could reach down and grab the meteorite out of the back of the car.

But before Marmalade could lift it, Wolf climbed onto the giant space rock and stood his ground. "Not so fast. Pull Snake up first. Or I'll use *this*." He pulled out the tube of lipstick he'd found in Diane's stash of gadgets.

"Oh, come now." Marmalade laughed.

With a flick of his wrist, Wolf converted the lipstick tube into a flame thrower and pointed the device at the cable dangling from the helicopter. He'd fry Marmalade's cable, and the meteorite would be toast. "Do it. Or you lose the rock!"

Wolf and Marmalade stared each other down. When it was clear neither of them was going to give up, Marmalade relented. "Okay, fine, if you insist. CUDDLES!" The chopper suddenly peeled upward into the sky, leaving Wolf far down below on the freeway. "You want him, he's yours." With that, he kicked Snake in the face and knocked him off the edge of the helicopter.

"Snake!" Wolf hollered as his best bud plummeted toward the ground.

Wolf had no choice but to leap off the meteorite and get behind the wheel. As soon as the cord was taut, the line attached to the meteorite lifted the giant rock up and out of the back of the Bad Guys' car. Marmalade had it again. But that no longer mattered since their friend was in serious danger. Catching Snake before he landed was all Wolf was thinking about now. They could deal with Marmalade and his meteorite later.

"Snake!" Piranha yelled while Wolf flicked the car into turbo mode.

"Oh no!" Shark cried as the car flew through wave after wave of guinea pigs. Snake was still twisting and spinning through the air, headed straight toward the Love Crater—the very spot the meteorite had hit not so long ago, which had set all this off in the first place. Wolf sped toward the crater, knowing they had no time to lose. But when they got close, the road was blocked off. There was a ROAD CLOSED sign marking the end of the broken highway where the meteorite had crashed through. They couldn't drive any farther.

"Guys, I know it's crazy—but we're going to jump it," Wolf told the others.

Piranha whooped. "Crazy? You're finally speaking my language, *chico*!"

Using the wave of guinea pigs as a sort of ramp, Wolf accelerated. They had to get as much air as they possibly could, or they'd never make the jump. Snake continued to fall, farther and farther down toward earth, as the Bad Guy mobile leaped off solid ground and flew up into the air toward him.

"We're gonna make it!" Piranha cheered. "We're gonna make it!" For one long second, it seemed like maybe Piranha was right. But then the reality of the jump hit them all, and it was obvious that they, too, were going down. The Love Crater was going to be the downfall of the Bad Guys. As they fell, Wolf swam through the air and caught Snake in his furry arms. If they were going down, they were going down *together*.

"You came back!" Snake said, shocked.

Wolf looked Snake in the eye and said, "Snake, I should have been honest with you. I was afraid that if you knew I wanted to be good, you'd—"

"—act like a jerk and never talk to you again?" Snake said, cutting him off.

"Basically." Wolf grinned. "The point is, I . . ."

"I love you, too," Snake said.

Shark began to weep—big, salty tears. "This is so beautiful. Do you know how beautiful this is? You guys?"

"Now you're gonna make *me* cry!" Piranha said, full-on weeping.

"I know," Tarantula said through tears. "So pathetic, right?"

Wolf beamed at his best friend, then turned to the other guys slyly. He slipped the grappling hook out of his suit and waved it in the air. "Come on. Who said this was the end?"

Just as the car slammed into the bottom of the crater, exploding on impact, Wolf wrapped his friends in his arms and sent the grappling hook flying. This time, it caught the edge of the crater.

While Marmalade watched on in horror from above, the Bad Guys flew out of the wreckage. The force from the blast knocked Marmalade off balance in the helicopter and blew the mind-control helmet off his head. It flew up and ricocheted off the tail rotor of the chopper. "No no no no—Cuddles!" Marmalade screamed. Without the mind-control helmet, the guinea pigs all *finally* deactivated and began turning back to normal. Meanwhile, the helicopter's injured tail rotor began to jerk and catch. "Uh-oh . . ." Marmalade said, his eyes going wide as the helicopter began to sputter.

Down below, Wolf was focused on getting his friends back to safety. While the others held tight to the rope attached to the grappling hook, Wolf climbed up onto the freeway ledge that their hook had caught when he activated it. As soon as he was back on solid ground, Wolf reached down and tugged his friends up beside him.

Suddenly, Piranha popped out from under Shark's butt, gasping for air. "What happened?" Piranha said. "Did we die? Is this heaven?"

But it was only heaven if *heaven* had the chief of police staring down at them, looking very much like she was going to lock them up for life. "That's it," the chief said as the Bad Guys emerged from the edge of the crater. "There is absolutely no way you're getting away this time!"

"Wait!" Diane said, stepping forward. "Chief!"

"Governor Foxington?" the chief said, spinning around.

"Don't do this!" she told her. "They didn't steal the meteorite; they were bringing it back!"

The police chief snorted. "Ha! How could you know that? Unless . . . unless you were conspiring with a bunch of known criminals?" She glanced suspiciously at the Bad Guys, then back at Diane.

Diane took a deep breath, then removed her glasses. "Well . . ." she began. "As a matter of fact, it's time I came clean about something. The truth is, I'm really . . . really—"

"—really a big fan of redemption arcs," Wolf interrupted. If Diane had successfully hid her criminal past for this long, he wasn't about to let her out herself. Why ruin the good thing she had going? "Yeah, Governor, we know."

Stunned, Diane turned and looked at Wolf, who had moved over to stand beside her. Wolf handed the cat from Marmalade's complex to Diane, then turned toward the police chief and lifted his paws. "We're done running away. Chief, do what you need to do."

The police chief was caught off guard. "You're . . . turning yourself in?"

"We might not have stolen the meteorite, but we did steal a lot of other things," Wolf admitted. "It's time we take responsibility and start a clean slate. Take us in, Chief." When the police chief didn't move, Wolf sighed and took the handcuffs himself.

"Wow," the chief said, stunned. "Really?"

Wolf slipped his hands into the cuffs and tightened them up. "You finally did it. This is your moment, Chief. Drink it in."

"Wow—I should . . . I should give a speech!" the chief said excitedly. "I should, shouldn't I?"

Wolf frowned. "Uh—"

But the chief was already pulling a crumpled, folded piece of paper from her pocket. She slid on her reading glasses and began her speech. "Ahem! When I was six years old, I decided that I wanted to play the piccolo—only to find that my fingers were just too powerful for that fragile little instrument. And that's when I discovered law enforcement—"

While she rambled on, Wolf and Diane exchanged knowing smiles. "I'm proud of you, Wolf," Diane said.

"You know," he told her. "A fox and a wolf are not that different. You've got a good thing going here, Governor."

Diane smiled thoughtfully, watching as the police loaded the Bad Guys into their vehicles.

Tiffany Fluffit had finally arrived on the scene. "The saga of the Bad Guys has come to a simple and totally satisfying conclusion," she said then, into the camera. "Though I wonder: What happened to the meteorite?" Tiffany's camera panned over, capturing footage of Marmalade sneaking the meteorite—still dangling from the belly of his helicopter—back to his compound. "Can it be?" Tiffany said excitedly, knowing she was possibly breaking the story of the century. "It's Professor Marmalade! He's bringing the meteorite back!"

Marmalade, realizing he was on camera, suddenly smiled and waved. He spun the helicopter around and waved again. "Yes!" he called out. "Yes, bringing it back! That's precisely what I'm doing!" The crowd gathered around the crater cheered and roared. "Look no further," Marmalade hollered. "Your hero has arrived!"

Wolf and the other Bad Guys exchanged a look. Was that annoying rodent seriously going to get away with this?

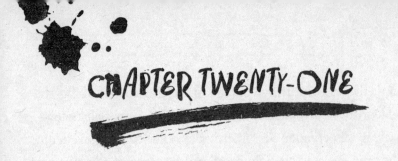

CHAPTER TWENTY-ONE

"Professor!" Tiffany cried out as Marmalade's helicopter landed, thrusting the news station's microphone in his face. "Care to comment?"

Marmalade posed smugly for the cameras. "I tried to help them, but in the end it's the same old story: bad guys bad, good guys good."

Tiffany nodded. "So true. So wise."

The guys and Diane watched Marmalade's performance, in total disbelief that someone could be *so* good at lying.

Marmalade spun to address the crowd. "Furthermore, for the good of the city, I have generously decided to take the meteorite back to my compound for safekeeping."

The Bad Guys were horrified, but the crowd was *totally* into this idea. They cheered, grateful for Marmalade's offer and relieved to have their hero back.

"Thank you," Marmalade gushed, bowing. "Gosh, you're kind. Give it up for *me*!" Marmalade clapped for himself. All of a sudden, the meteorite turned off . . . then on . . . then off again.

Everyone stared. What on Earth was going on?

"Wait a sec!" the police chief cried. "This isn't the meteorite! It's a lamp!"

There was a din of conversation as everyone turned to ask the person standing next to them what on Earth was going on.

That's when Snake began to chuckle. "Hehehehe." There was a big, fat secret he'd been keeping from *everyone*. See, the thing was, Snake loved his friends. He just didn't like to *tell* them that. But when he'd shared that one remaining push pop with Shark and put someone else's needs above his own, it *had* made him feel good—and that's when he'd realized he really wasn't ready to leave his friends after all. He'd felt the wag, and it was incredible.

But by *pretending* to leave the Bad Guys, Snake had realized, he could help his pals!

He explained to everyone that he'd joined Marmalade as partner and set his clever plan in action. After he gained Marmalade's trust, he had taken his turn with the mind-control helmet—but instead of using the helmet to carry out Marmalade's plan, Snake had mind-controlled the guinea pigs to carry out *his* plan: to spray-paint the lamp replica of the meteorite so it would look exactly like the real thing. Then he had the rodents swap it out, real for fake, knowing his pals would come to try to steal it.

"But . . ." Marmalade said, cutting him off. He pointed to the "meteorite" and asked, "If that's a lamp, where is the—"

Snake giggled. "Hehehe, the ol' switcheroo." He told everyone how the guinea pigs had swapped the real one for the fake one, then turned the *real* meteorite's dials from STABLE to UNSTABLE, then all the way to SYSTEM OVERLOAD.

The meteorite had some exploding to do.

Just as Snake snapped his fingers, a giant ball of flames shot up into the sky from way across the city. The news cameras zoomed in, catching the Golden Dolphin flying up into the sky. It appeared that Snake—and the *real* meteorite—had blown up Professor Marmalade's evil compound!

"Noooooooo!" Marmalade screamed, folding over in despair.

"Whoo!" Shark cheered. "That's my reptile, right there!"

Piranha buzzed with happiness.

"C'mon," Snake said modestly. "Somebody had to destroy the meteorite. That thing was dangerous!"

The Bad Guys hopped into the back of the poli car. They were ready to get back to the city and ride story out. They knew they were going to have to do hard time for all the things they'd stolen over the years they knew it was the right thing to do.

"That was pretty good, Snakey!" Wolf told his pal a

zipped away from Marmalade, the cameras, and the crater.

"C'mon," Snake said, looking side-eyed at him. "It was genius. Not only did I foil the pig, I got *you* to admit how much you care about me."

"And I thought we weren't supposed to make things personal," Wolf pointed out.

"It worked, didn't it?" Snake said. "The look on your face when you realized that meteorite was the lamp!" He kissed his fingertips. "Priceless!"

Wolf suddenly had a sly glint in his eye. "Sure, yeah . . . I just wonder about one little thing."

"Oh yeah?" Snake said, tentative. "What's that, Wolf?"

Wolf smiled cockily. "Who do you think put that *one* push pop in the fridge for you to find?"

Snake's eyes widened. "Wait, you . . . noooooo!" He'd been *had*! Tricked. Conned!

"I knew you were good deep down," Wolf told him with a smile. He popped his sunglasses on as the police car zipped through the streets.

"We're *good*, baby!" Webs whooped. "We're good!"

Wolf grinned. The gang was back!

CHAPTER TWENTY-TWO

Back at the edge of the Love Crater, Marmalade was mourning all that he had lost that day. His compound, his heist, his *meteorite*. Suddenly, the Golden Dolphin dropped out of the sky and hit the fake meteorite square on. The meteorite lamp shook and wobbled from the force of the impact, then fell right onto Professor Marmalade, trapping him. "Ahh!" Marmalade wailed.

He dug and scrambled, trying to get free, but in the scuffle, Diane's Zumpango Diamond ring fell out of his pocket and onto the ground in front of all the reporters and people gathered around.

The police chief lifted it up, inspecting the ring closely. "Hold on . . ." she said. "This is the Zumpango Diamond! But this was stolen"—she gasped, staring at Professor Marmala[de] in a whole new light—"by the Crimson Paw!"

"Me?!" Marmalade shrieked. "You think *I'm* the Cri[mson] Paw? Oh no—no no no—you've got it wrong!"

But the police chief wasn't going to be duped yet a[gain]. She grabbed Marmalade and tossed him into the back [seat.]

own police wagon. She slammed the door shut and drove off—happy to have one *more* bad guy locked up.

Tiffany Fluffit stared as the police chief drove off with Marmalade in captivity. "OMG, in a shocking twist, the notorious bandit known as 'The Crimson Paw' has been revealed to be none other than Professor Marmalade!"

"No no no!" Marmalade screamed out the window of the police wagon. He pointed at Diane, who was watching with an amused expression. "I'm not the Crimson Paw—*she's* the Crimson Paw! SHE'S THE PAWWWWW! I'm the flower of goodness!"

CHAPTER TWENTY-THREE

(One Year Later)

(Sentence Reduction for Good Behavior)

"Okay," Wolf said to Snake as they headed out of prison—finally *free*—a year after the whole meteorite thing. "So, imagine it's your birthday—"

Snake cut him off. "It *is* my birthday."

"Yeah, I know. But you're walking along and you meet a genie—" Wolf went on.

"What's his name?" Snake asked.

"What's the genie's name?" Wolf lifted one brow.

"I wanna know who I'm talking to," Snake explained as he grabbed his bag of personal items off the counter befor leaving the jail, heading back out into fresh air and freed

"I dunno," Wolf said, shrugging. "'Genie.' Or 'Gen short. So, he offers you three wishes."

"Okay," Snake said. "Why three?"

Wolf said, "You know, industry standard. Now, w you wish for?"

"I'm gonna go with . . ." Snake thought for a second. "Nothing."

"Nothing?" Wolf balked. "Come on . . . it's your birthday."

Snake shook his head. "What do I need wishes for? I got my freedom—" Snake and Wolf pushed through a door, out into the prison yard, while Snake continued to count off his blessings.

"I've got my friends—" Snake continued.

In the prison yard, the other three Bad Guys joined them. "Hey!" Webs cried out.

"Guys!" Shark whooped.

"Looking good, amigos!" Piranha said.

Snake finished up his list of blessings. "And I've got the skin of a reptile half my age."

"I don't know about half your age, but you do look good," Shark said.

"Well," Wolf said, grinning, "that's because you just molted."

"Yes, I did!" Snake said.

"You smell good, too," Shark told him.

"I'm shiny." Snake beamed. "I'm gorgeous."

Together, the five Bad Guys headed for the prison gates. Their tails, fins, and bellies were wagging with excitement good feelings as they stepped past the fence and into bright, free world. But as soon as they got outside, the reality of their situation hit them like a five-ton meteorite. "Sooo . . . what do we do now?" Shark said quietly.

"Steal a car?" Piranha suggested.

"Piranha!" Webs scolded.

Piranha shrank under the angry looks of the others. "I was *joking*. It was a joke."

Snake glanced at Wolf. "You know, on second thought, Wolf, maybe I'd wish for a ride."

Wolf grinned. That was more like it. "Oh yeah? *Alakazam!*" On those words, there was a screech of tires and an instant later the Bad Guy mobile pulled up to the curb in front of them. Diane was at the wheel!

"Nice," Snake mused.

Diane rolled down the window. "Hey, guys," Diane said with a smile. "Ready to get to work?"

The cat from Marmalade's compound hopped out of the car and into Wolf's arms. "Hey!" Wolf said with a laugh. "Whoa!"

The former Bad Guys all piled into the car. Diane s[lid] over so Wolf could take his usual spot at the wheel. [Wolf] grinned as he settled into his seat. He dropped his sung[lasses] over his eyes and winked at Diane. "Webs, hit it!" As so[on as] the music came pouring out of the car's speakers, Wolf fl[oored] it. It felt good to be back where he belonged, with his favorite pack.